THE Afterlife Academy

THE Afterlife Academy

FRANK L. COLE

DELACORTE PRESS

Text copyright © 2015 by Frank L. Cole
Jacket art copyright © 2015 by Lisa Weber

All rights reserved. Published in the United States by Delacorte Press,
an imprint of Random House Children's Books, a division of
Penguin Random House LLC, New York.

Delacorte Press is a registered trademark and the colophon is
a trademark of Penguin Random House LLC.

Visit us on the Web! randomhousekids.com

Educators and librarians, for a variety of teaching tools,
visit us at RHTeachersLibrarians.com

Library of Congress Cataloging-in-Publication Data
Cole, Frank.
The Afterlife Academy / Frank L. Cole. — First edition.
pages cm.
Summary: A twelve-year-old boy and his Guardian Agent,
sent from The Afterlife Academy on his first mission, must work together
and save Earth from an eclectic horde of blundering enemies.
ISBN 978-0-385-74481-2 (hc) — ISBN 978-0-385-39147-4 (ebook)
ISBN 978-0-375-99186-8 (glb)
[1. Future life—Fiction. 2. Dead—Fiction. 3. Schools—Fiction.] I. Title.
PZ7.C673435Af 2015 [Fic]—dc23 2014028078

The text of this book is set in 12-point Minion.
Jacket design by Katrina Damkoehler
Interior design by Heather Kelly

Printed in the United States of America
10 9 8 7 6 5 4 3 2 1
First Edition

FOR HEIDI,
WHO LISTENS WHEN I READ
AND STAYS AWAKE

Disturbing News

Walter Prairie was weeding his family's garden as punishment for punching the neighbor bully in the lip, when his world lit up with a bright white flash. It happened so suddenly, he barely had time to blink. He felt a warm breeze and heard the sound of soft music as his surroundings blurred, then disappeared.

When he opened his eyes, he looked down, expecting still to be holding the garden trowel. But it was gone. Then he noticed how pink and clean his skin looked. His nails glowed.

"What the—" Walter yelped as he held his fingers close to his eyes, trying to focus. Someone was going to get slugged for painting his nails.

Walter glanced around and realized that he was in an office. It looked like a principal's office. What was he doing there?

Brightly lit hallways stretched endlessly from the room.

He could see no fewer than a hundred closed doors along either side. Unless his school had recently gone through a remodel without him being aware of it, this wasn't the principal's office at Yorkshire Middle School. And what was with the strange harplike music playing in the background? Walter cocked his head to the side, listening to what sounded like the Tasty Nibs cat food commercial. He could almost see the weird disembodied cat head bouncing across the screen as he sang the jingle in his mind.

Tasty Nibs, Tasty Nibs. Keep your paws off, I got dibs. Mee-ow.

"Please state your name and age." A voice snapped Walter out of his daze. A squirrelly-looking man with dark-rimmed glasses sat at a desk, where a tower of brown folders teetered almost to the ceiling.

Walter jiggled his pinky in his ear. "Huh?"

"Your name and age." The man pulled a folder from the middle of the tower.

"Dude!" Flinching, Walter stuck out his hands to keep the folders from toppling. The tower swayed precariously from left to right, but no folders fell. Not even the ones from the tip-top. "My name's Walter," he mumbled. "I'm twelve."

The man snapped his fingers impatiently. "Your full name, Walter. Chop-chop. I need to make sure we have a match."

"A match for what?" Walter asked. The man pressed the tips of his fingers together and flared his nostrils. "Okay, okay. I'm Walter Prairie. Who are you?"

"*I* am Alton Tremonton." The man forced out the words without separating his teeth. "And you, Walter Prairie, are dead."

2

A Shady Gathering

Charlie Dewdle knelt on top of a massive dirt pile behind the condemned shopping mall on Victory Junction. He was a thin boy with pale, freckled skin and a shock of messy, bright red—almost orange—hair. Above him, wilted gray clouds gathered in the warm autumn sky. The weatherman had predicted rain yet again. It would be the third storm in six days. The quiet city of Gabbiter, Iowa, had never been so wet.

A bright green blip appeared on the screen of Charlie's electromagnetic field detector as he scanned the large hole he had just discovered. Charlie knew all about the ins and outs of EMF. He had read many books on the subject and had even taken an online class on how to use his detector to track ghosts.

Charlie pressed "record" on his video camera, which was positioned on a tripod near the hole, then stepped into view of the lens, still holding the EMF detector.

"At precisely"—he checked his watch—"four-thirty p.m., following a tip from a reliable source, I, Charlie Dewdle, discovered what appears to be the burial site of the notorious Friedman Salinger."

There had been no reliable source, and Charlie didn't really believe the hole held the grave of Friedman Salinger, the long-dead Colton County strangler. But no one in the paranormally inclined world cared about empty, boring holes. His video needed a little drama before he submitted it to his favorite website. Besides, who knew?

Demolition on the shopping mall property had ceased two months earlier, when the mayor of Gabbiter had informed the public that part of the building was a historic landmark. It had been brought to the mayor's attention that the eastern wing, which once housed the movie theater, was older than the town itself.

"It is my civic duty to prevent the further demolition of such a cherished piece of history," Mayor Tungsten had said in his television interview. "Who knows what sorts of memories will be found down there? Until we invest our energies in uncovering them, construction on the new water park will be postponed."

Most of Charlie's classmates hated the mayor for making that announcement. The Typhoon Water Park was going to have seven epic water slides, a lazy river for rafting, and the second-largest wave pool in the central United States.

But Charlie hated swimming. He sunburned too easily and didn't enjoy the taste of chlorine. The water park could wait. Especially since historic stone structures were almost always hot spots for lingering ghosts and spirits.

"As you can see, the electromagnetic readings are off the charts," Charlie said into the camera. Digging in his backpack, he pulled out his helmet flashlight and fastened it atop his messy red hair. "Time to see what ol' Salinger wanted to keep hidden from the world."

Charlie lay on his stomach and directed the headlamp into the darkness. The hole sank at least six feet underground. Charlie's skin prickled. Something down that deep really could mean a burial plot. *Salinger's burial plot.* The light from his helmet glinted off the corner of something at the bottom, and he leaned forward for a better view.

"Ahoy!" Charlie hollered, then checked over his shoulder to make sure no one had heard. It was a book. It had a dark cover and metal cornerpieces.

Taking great care to keep from falling, Charlie descended into the hole and pulled the book from its resting place. It had to be at least a hundred years old. The cover was worn and cracked, the pages thick and waxy. Charlie narrowed his eyes as he carefully dusted the cover free of grime and attempted to read the title. But the words were in some foreign language.

Charlie noticed that the EMF detector was burping as several green circles appeared on the screen. He smacked the monitor with his hand. "Worthless piece of—" He froze midsentence and stared back at the book. Taking the EMF detector in his hand, he grazed it over the cover. The circles of green light grew brighter. He flipped the book over. The lights quivered, and the detector suddenly made an unusual *whop-whop-whop*ping sound. Charlie grinned, but in his stomach he felt a tiny tingle of fear. He couldn't understand why, since finding something mysterious at the bottom of a hole should've filled him with joy.

Perhaps it was because Charlie was no longer alone.

At that very moment, three dark spirits from the Underworld—shades, as they preferred to be called—were gathering around him.

3

A Strange Realization

"I'm dead?" Walter gnawed on his lip. *I'm dead.* Somehow, he knew it was true. He didn't know why it made sense, but it did.

"Yep. Sorry." Alton made a frowny face. The kind that people made when they didn't really feel sorry at all. Scrunched nose. Puckered lips. Walter wanted to punch it off Alton's face, but slugging an adult, even a puny, rude one perched behind a desk, wasn't a great idea.

"How come I'm not sad or anything? And why don't I miss my parents?" Walter asked.

"Because you've gone through a *Cleansing.* Standard procedure. It helps you move on without any grief."

"I don't remember any . . . cleansing." Did they wash everyone in a big bathtub after they died? That would explain his pinkish skin and glossy fingernails. Walter glanced up at the wall behind Alton's desk and stared at a clock in the shape of a pig wearing a bow tie and a party hat. Though there were numbers on the clock indicating the different hours of the day, there wasn't a minute or a second hand.

"Of course you don't." Alton massaged the wrinkles in his brow with his fingers. "Who would want to remember a three-day mourning period? The memory of your Cleansing has been completely erased from your mind. Dead people no longer have to worry about things like their families and such."

Walter stared down at his body and saw the same clothing he had been wearing while out in the garden: a red-and-white-striped shirt with denim shorts that stopped below his knees, and scuffed sneakers.

"This is what you wear when you're dead?" He tugged at the end of his shirt.

Alton leaned forward. "That is what *you* wear."

"Forever?"

"Could be worse," Alton mumbled, returning his attention to Walter's file. "You could be wearing that awful outfit your parents buried you in this morning. Chocolate-brown pants and a paisley tie." Alton shuddered.

Walter's eyes narrowed as he began to concoct a rude comeback, but he decided it wasn't worth it. "So what do I do now?"

"Now? You are Categorized, and then you must complete a questionnaire based on your chosen Category. Two thousand questions. All very critical to your eventual placement within your Category—or another, if you are deemed unsuitable for your choice."

"A pop quiz with two thousand questions?" Walter

squeaked. "That's ridiculous! What is this place? It doesn't sound like heaven."

Alton smiled and continued. "Oh, right. Your report did mention your aptitude for grasping new ideas was a little low. This isn't heaven."

"It's not?" Walter wondered if he had somehow ticked off the wrong guy. "Then is it . . ."

"No, it isn't that place either. Seriously, do I look like someone who would be employed in the other location?" Alton sighed exhaustedly. "This is a Categorizing Office. Not everyone goes here when they die, but some souls do. I tend to see a lot of youths, athletes, and geniuses. Obviously, you are the foremost." He examined his fingernails for a moment. "So, is it all clear now?"

Walter shook his head. "No! It doesn't make any sense. If I'm really dead, why didn't I go to heaven? I've been *mostly* good, haven't I?"

Alton shrugged and slid a thick binder across the desk. "I don't know, and I don't care. That's not my job. But if it makes you feel any better, ninety-nine percent of the folks who pass through a Categorizing Office will eventually end up in heaven. It's the decision of the higher-ups"—Alton raised his eyes to the ceiling and jabbed his pointer finger toward it—"to give you the opportunity to be useful until you're ready. There are many fields of expertise from which you may choose, although I must point out that you're not guaranteed a spot in any of them."

While Alton spoke, Walter examined the binder. Each page contained a bold heading describing a job performed by individuals in the Afterlife and a list of its requirements. One of the categories was titled *Counseling the Confused*. Centered on the page just beneath the heading was a picture of a woman lying on a couch while another woman sat in a large wingback chair, in a state of pondering. Walter read the description.

> Many of the Recently Departed require extra attention after their Cleansing. Some poor souls find it difficult to let go and move on. They need a shoulder to cry on, a willing ear to listen, or a bold voice of reason. Those with social work backgrounds or a degree in psychology are certain to find this assignment both enriching and rewarding.

"What the heck?" Walter muttered. "Who would want to be a guidance counselor for dead people?"

There were more than fifty different Categories, including Dead Pet Foster Care, Celestial Construction, Heavenly Choir Participant, and . . .

"Grim Reaper Assistant?" Walter gulped.

"Ah, then you have chosen a Category," Alton said, smiling. "Excellent choice."

"No! I was just reading out loud." Walter hastily continued flipping through the pages. "So let me get this straight. I'm supposed to choose one of these jobs, and then I have to do it for a few years, and then I go to heaven?"

"Sounds to me like you finally understand. Well done!"

Alton's voice dripped with sarcasm. "Now, perhaps we could get on with it sometime this decade."

Walter closed the book and slid it a few inches back in Alton's direction. "What's heaven like?"

"How should I know?"

"Oh. Did you just die too?"

"Did I just *die*?" Alton echoed in disbelief. "Absurd!"

"Well, why haven't you gone there yet?" Walter pried. "Were you one of the one percent that didn't make it?"

"I most certainly was not!" Alton huffed. "We all have jobs to do, and some of our jobs take us longer to complete."

"Don't you ever take a break and go check it out?"

Alton's eyes narrowed. "I do *not* take breaks. In fifty years at my post, I have never taken a single break."

Just then, one of the doors down the left hallway opened, and three young boys, maybe a year older than Walter, appeared and began walking toward him.

A Narrow Escape

Evil had the same effect on shades as pimiento cheese sandwiches had on Charlie. Its delicious aroma drew them in.

Charlie couldn't hear the shades, or see them, for that matter, but he felt cold. The hairs on his neck quivered as one of the dark spirits moved right next to him, floating mere inches from his ear. Charlie rubbed his arms.

"Why doesn't the boy open the book?" it whispered. Shades, while low on the Underworld totem pole, did have impressive powers of persuasion.

Charlie opened the book, and the shades fell silent as they began to read. Then, all at once, they released a collective gasp.

"What is this?" one asked with giddiness in its throat.

"It has so much power!" said another.

As they swirled around Charlie, the lights on the EMF detector danced feverishly.

Charlie closed the book and gulped. He had to get home.

Cramming all his belongings, including the strange book, into his backpack, Charlie raced down the dirt hill. As he rounded the corner onto Victory Junction, he plowed face-first into something large and alive. It was Mo Horvath. The meanest guy in school.

"What are the odds?" Charlie groaned.

"Hey, guys, look at this turd!" Mo clasped his meaty fingers around the scruff of Charlie's neck. "It's Charlie Doo-doodle."

A chorus of snickers erupted. "Yeah! It's Charlie Poople!" said Wheeler, by far the most idiotic of the bunch.

Mo sneered at Wheeler. "Not *Poople*, stupid. It's Doo-doodle."

Wheeler blinked in confusion, and Charlie desperately searched for a gap to shimmy his way through.

"Yes, it's me," Charlie said, sucking on his teeth. Mo had given Charlie the nickname Doo-doodle at the beginning of the school year. It wasn't growing on him.

"My lucky day, huh?" Mo elbowed Wheeler's side and squeezed Charlie's neck. "Guess what time it is?"

Charlie sniffed the air and squinted. "Uh . . . I'm guessing, shower time?"

Charlie should have known that insults did not sit well with Mo, but he was trying to stall.

Mo flicked Charlie's ear with his fat finger. "Think you're funny?" He shoved Charlie toward Oswald, a gangly, pimpled boy, who finagled Charlie into a perfect full nelson. A full nelson was a wrestling move that, on television, tended to be fake. In real life, it pinched something awful. "Here I was thinking I wouldn't get to finish football practice."

Mo stood well over five feet tall and had a fat midsection, wide shoulders, and thick biceps. He also wore his blond hair in a flattop. Only the really tough kids could pull off a flattop without getting picked on. And Mo's flattop had perfectly sharp edges glistening with hair gel.

"Check his bag," Wheeler sneered.

Mo snatched the backpack from Charlie's shoulders and yanked open the zipper. The EMF detector and Charlie's video equipment fell to the sidewalk, shattering into several pieces. "Oops," Mo said with a chuckle.

Charlie's eyes burned with tears. "Don't you have some cigarettes to go steal?"

"What's this? Your diary?" Mo pulled the old book from the pocket and shoved the empty backpack into Charlie's hands.

"Open it," Wheeler said eagerly. "Open it."

Mo opened the cover just as the florist across the street stepped out onto the sidewalk and glared at the group. "What are you doing to that boy?" She marched over, her hands clenched at her sides. Mo turned his head, and Charlie yanked the book from Mo's hands. He had no time to collect his other belongings, but they were broken anyway. Charlie took off down the sidewalk.

The boys gave chase until the road split in two directions, and then gave up. Charlie could hear them firing off insults as he slowed his pace and chanced a wary glance back in their direction. The gang of bullies had already turned, continuing down Victory Junction.

On Dupont Avenue, right across the street from the Kindhearted Veterinary Clinic, Charlie ascended the four crumbling stone stairs that led to his family's apartment complex. As he fumbled with his keys, the clinic exploded with barking and wailing dogs. This was nothing unusual. They always barked whenever Charlie walked past, which always upset Charlie's birds—all seven of them, to be exact. There were four canaries, two finches, and one very old blue parakeet that no longer chirped but instead made a sound similar to the noise a car made when it backfired. For reasons Charlie had never figured out, all dogs hated his birds, and they hated him because they could smell the feather dust on his clothing.

Charlie finally got inside and locked the door behind him. Outside, thunder boomed, and through the thin walls of the apartment, Charlie could hear rain beginning to fall.

Categorized

The boys who had just entered Alton's office wore stark white military-type uniforms, complete with white boots, a white beret, and a white utility belt. Their voices carried high-spirited tones of excitement, and they chatted with one another as though they were up to some wonderful plan.

"Hey, hey! What's up, Al?" one of the boys asked, smacking Alton's back.

"Ronald," Alton replied, offering a forced smile as he swatted Ronald's hand away from Walter's file. "Where are you off to?"

"We've just been *assigned*." Ronald rubbed the top of his hand.

"Ah, yes, I was told. And I suppose you need your Access Portals?" Alton scratched his nose. "Oh, joy. A trio of fresh Agents, out to save the world."

"That's the idea," Ronald answered.

Alton opened a drawer and removed three tiny objects

that looked like miniature white paper clips. "Here you go. We wouldn't want you to forget these and end up stuck on earth, now, would we?"

The boys took the clips from Alton and fastened them to their belts.

"Who's the newbie?" Ronald flicked his chin in a friendly gesture toward Walter.

Alton frowned as one of the other boys successfully swiped the folder from the desk and began to leaf through the pages. "Give that back, Reginald!" His voice rose with agitation.

"'Walter Prairie,'" Reginald read. "'Died Thursday by . . .'" He paused to reread the data. "Whoa, check it out!" He flashed the file to Ronald and the other boy.

"Lightning?" Ronald asked after reading Walter's file. "Is this for real?"

"I was struck by lightning?" Walter scoffed as he leaned over the file and read the blurb. "Died while weeding in his mother's herb garden." What a sad way to go. Picking strangler weeds out of the chives. Those were the worst. Chives always made Walter's hands smell weird.

"Awesome! My name's Ronald," Ronald said, extending his hand and staring at Walter with admiration. "And this is Reginald and Riley. We're the Logan brothers." Walter glanced at all three boys as he shook their hands, noticing the similarities between them. "We're triplets. Fraternal. But we didn't die in a cool way like you."

"How did *you* die?" Walter asked.

"Smoke inhalation," Riley muttered. "Lame. We died in our sleep, which is even lamer."

"That sounds awful." Dying from suffocation had to be a terrible way to go.

Ronald glanced at the pig clock on the wall. "Yikes, we gotta go."

"Where are you guys going?" Walter followed Ronald's gaze, wondering how he could tell time on a clock with no hands.

"These boys have been assigned as Afterlife Academy Agents." Alton twirled his finger in the air. "It's perhaps the most boring way to spend the eternities."

Ronald looked at Walter, grinning from ear to ear. "It rocks, dude! We've been given important human targets and high-level missions to protect them." The other two nodded in unison, eyes wide with excitement.

"'Important human targets'?" Walter said. "What are you guys, like guardian angels or something?"

"The correct term is Guardian *Agent*. Or Afterlife Academy Agent. We're not angels yet," said Riley.

"So you go on missions?"

"Yeah, man." Ronald playfully socked Walter in the arm. He stuck a hand in one of the compartments of his utility belt and pulled out a small, laminated card. "'Tyrone Underhill,'" he read. "'Only son of Sheldon Underhill, CEO of Carmichael Armored Vehicles.'"

Following suit, the other brothers pulled out their own laminated cards.

"Harold Jenkins," Riley said. "Grandson of the infamous Myra Jenkins of Jenkins, Poindexter, and Puffins criminal-law firm."

"Max Meridian, oldest son of Bruno Meridian, head accountant for the Pomadoro Syndicate, the most notorious crime family in Michigan," Reginald finished.

The three brothers exchanged loud high fives.

"Why do you have to protect them?" Walter asked. Important human targets. Secret missions. Utility belts! It was like James Bond.

"Because of who their parents are," Ronald answered. "It makes them targets for the enemies. You know—demons and their Underworld minions. Wraiths. Shades. Their whole existence is centered on invading earth and wreaking havoc. They hate humans and will do anything in their power to cause chaos. These kids have parents who are involved in some pretty dangerous work. If the demons can in any way gain control over something like a criminal organization, they could do some serious damage. That's why they go after the kids. Kids can be easily turned with a little demonic persuasion. If we don't step in and protect our targets, terrible things could happen."

Walter swallowed. Demons? Wraiths? He'd never believed in those sorts of things. "How'd you guys get that job?"

"They enrolled in the Afterlife Academy," Alton said.

"You can do that?" Being an Afterlife Academy Agent sounded frightening and yet, somewhat intriguing. Walter would much rather do what they were doing than be forced to bounce around the clouds like a Care Bear or clean up after Grim Reapers.

"Well." Alton's voice rose as he stared at the ceiling. "Technically you can, but the Academy has plenty of Agents as it stands. You'll just add to the overcrowding. I suggest you choose a more fitting Category. The Heavenly Choir is in desperate need of a few hearty baritones."

Walter groaned. He had once been forced by his mother to participate in the school choral production. He didn't exactly have the voice of an angel.

"Don't listen to him!" Ronald interjected, stepping between Walter and Alton. "Anyone who's been struck by lightning is the type of Agent the Academy's looking for."

Walter pumped his fist. Had he still been alive and showing this much interest in attending school, he felt certain his parents would have choked on their own tongues. He hated school. Despised his teachers. Loathed the principal. But this was different from regular school.

"Where do I sign up? Can I go with you guys?" he asked.

"Ha!" Alton pulled Ronald out of his way to glare at Walter. "We haven't even started your questionnaire, and the Afterlife Academy takes at least four years to complete. *'Can I go with you guys?'*" he mimicked.

"Four *years*?" Walter groaned. Maybe he should reconsider this.

"Yeah, but the time flies. And you need the training," Riley said.

"What sort of training?"

"Shade Spotting and Hand-to-Hand Combat," Reginald began.

"Thought Whispering and Energy Transfer," Riley continued.

"Shielding and Animal Communication," Ronald finished. "There's a lot. But the instructors are awesome, and you'll breeze through the courses in no time. Well, take it easy, Walter, and remember, have fun and soak up as much as you can." With that, the Logan brothers charged through the second door down the right hallway.

"Ahem." Alton slid a thick packet of papers across his desk. "It is the most difficult questionnaire of them all to complete, but that was your choice." Walter picked up the questionnaire and a pencil and glanced at the cover sheet. "It's not all fun and games, you know," Alton continued, "the Afterlife Academy. In fact, you'll probably drop out in a month."

Walter ignored him and eagerly began the arduous process of completing the questionnaire.

SpiritSpy.org

C harlie entered his family's study. Within the slightly cramped quarters of the room, Mr. Dewdle had set up a computer desk, a reclining office chair, and a ratty-looking futon. The rest of the office belonged to Charlie's birds. Upon seeing him enter, the canaries and finches tweeted anxiously and pecked at their cages with their beaks. The ancient blue parakeet in the corner of the room cocked its head to the side and gave a rattling squawk. Charlie shushed them by dribbling handfuls of minuscule pellets into their feed bowls.

Charlie sat down at the computer, entered the screen-saver password, and connected to the Internet. Within a few seconds, he had navigated to one of his favorite websites: SpiritSpy.org. The website was run by Wisdom Willows, a giant in the world of paranormal enthusiasts.

Charlie clicked the `Chat with Wisdom` link at the top of the screen and entered his question.

```
I found a book in a hole. It's writ-
ten in some foreign language, and when
I picked it up, my EMF detector went
crazy. Is that normal? How often do
books register high readings on EMF de-
tectors?
```

He hit "send" just as the sound of his mother clinking the silverware at the kitchen table announced dinner. He would have to wait to see if Wisdom Willows would respond.

7

The Afterlife Academy

After nearly two hours of absolute boredom, Walter painfully scribbled the last answer of Alton's two-thousand-question questionnaire. Never in his life had he been so relieved to finish an exam.

"Can I go now?" he asked.

"There's still time to change your mind," Alton said. "Think about it. You could be singing with the Heavenly Choir. Their concerts are the stuff of legends." He gazed over Walter's shoulder and his vision blurred.

"Tempting," Walter said, standing from his chair. "But I think I'll pass."

Alton clucked his tongue and refocused his eyes. "Suit yourself. It's the second-to-last door before the end." Alton gestured toward the left side of the left hallway.

The wooden doors that lined the hall looked like they led to classrooms. Each of them was numbered with gold-flaked lettering above the doorframe and had a frosted square window. Walter arrived at his designated door, but a fluttery sensation in his chest caused him to hesitate before turning the knob. It was like the first day of school all over again. Were there things like detention or suspension at the Afterlife Academy? Walter could almost hear his father's timeless advice just behind his ear.

Don't be stupid.

Squeezing the knob in his fingers, Walter gazed back down the hallway and jumped.

Alton was right behind him. "Is it locked?" he asked.

"Uh . . . I don't think so."

"Course not. Now go!"

Walter opened the door.

Warm sunlight pressed through the opening as he stepped onto a landing. A row of at least twenty marble steps descended to a grassy arena where hundreds of men and women were engaged in a variety of unusual activities. A group of uniformed cadets wove their way through an obstacle course. They sidestepped and somersaulted past large, monster-shaped targets that appeared out of nowhere, then climbed a rock wall and rappelled down the other side.

Walter grabbed for the handrail to steady his legs as the door behind him latched shut. "What is this place?"

Just beyond the last marble step, a small gathering of children standing with an instructor extended their hands in unison, fingers pointed toward a turquoise sky.

"Remember your training!" the instructor shouted, projecting his voice loud enough that the children could hear him above the bustling sounds of exercises carrying on throughout the arena.

The children nodded. Some of them closed their eyes tight in concentration, while a few others stuck out their tongues. Purple lights suddenly enveloped each of them. The children looked like giant, perfectly round soap bubbles. Walter laughed as the bubbles quivered and, after a few moments, burst.

"Well done!" the instructor praised. "You've successfully conjured your first shield." He applauded, then noticed Walter gawking at the top of the stairs. "You there. Have you checked in yet?" The man pointed toward a long row of people weaving their way to some distant tables.

Walter fell in line behind a large woman he almost mistook for a man. She was tall and burly, but by no means fat, and wore some sort of sports jersey. She glanced over her shoulder and noticed Walter staring at the numbers on her back.

"Name's Urga," she grunted. "I played forward in women's rugby for the Melbourne Murderers." Her voice was laced with a thick Australian accent. "Died in a scrum."

"Oh." Walter raised his eyebrows to show interest, but had no clue what a scrum was. "What's going on out here?"

"It's Field Day. Happens once a week. Cadets are given several hours to test out what they've learned in a safe, controlled environment. Should be loads of fun."

"Did Alton tell you about Field Day?" Walter asked.

"Who? Don't know no Alton."

"The guy from the Categorizing Office. He wears glasses. Has a pig clock on the wall behind his desk. Kinda mean."

Urga shrugged and spat a loogie on the sidewalk. "S'pose there's more than one Categorizer in this place. Don't you think?"

Alton's office had been empty when Walter arrived. Certainly it would have been swarming with other dead people if he were the only Categorizer. Urga made sense.

The arena was bigger than any stadium Walter had ever seen. "Where does the Heavenly Choir sing? In those bleachers?" Not that he really cared about that.

"The choir's down another door, but that's for wussies. All of this belongs to the Academy. It's the only Guardian Agent program in the Afterlife."

Walter's eyes drifted along the slow-moving line of new recruits. Men, women, boys, and girls shuffled a few steps at a time, but Walter couldn't see the end of it.

"Where does this go?" he asked Urga.

"Check-in. They assign us into dormitories, give us uniforms, schedules, you know, all that."

"Whoa! Is that a tank?" A motorized machine made of see-through metal crawled into view, its tracks chewing up clods of grass and dirt. A woman wearing white fatigues, like everyone else on the lawn, sat with her upper body poking through the open hatch of the tank. After aiming an enormous cannon, she fired a purple missile at a target at least five hundred yards south of the arena. The concussive boom of the cannon sent Walter barreling to the ground with his hands shielding his head.

Urga appeared unfazed.

"That . . . was . . . awesome! Do we get to drive those?"

Urga shrugged and turned to face forward. Clearly the

question-and-answer portion of their time together had ended.

An hour later, Urga had made fast friends with a portly Viking named Gordon, and the two were discussing the pros and cons of penalty-inducing blocking in "American" football. Walter was pretty sure the Viking was just wearing a costume, but the beard looked real enough.

The wide banquet tables were finally only a few yards away, when a man carrying a clipboard approached Walter.

"You there. Are you Walter Prairie?"

"Uh . . . yeah. That's me." Walter stood on his tiptoes to see over the edge of the clipboard, but the man hid it from view.

"You lived at Two Thirty-Seven Poleman Boulevard in Baldwin, Virginia?"

"That *was* my address." Walter smirked. "Until I . . ."

"Son of Greg and Darlene Prairie and older brother to—"

"Dude, I said it was me!" What was with the clipboard and the questions?

"This way, sir." The man held his hand out toward the front of the line.

Sir? When had he ever been called sir? "Why? Where are we going?"

The man had already pushed off, walking briskly past the row of tables. Walter hopped out of line and hurried to keep up.

"What is this about? I thought I was supposed to check in at that table." Had the Academy reached its capacity? The thought tied his stomach in knots. They couldn't ask him to leave now. Not after he'd seen people shooting purple light missiles!

"Did I do something wrong?"

"Just come with me, please."

Reluctantly, Walter continued to follow the man. Eventually, the walkway they were on rounded a corner and ended at an office door, which the man opened. Black and white tiles formed a checkerboard across the floor of the room inside, and dark wooden bookshelves lined the walls. A statue of a full-sized lion crouched in the corner behind an immense oak desk, where a man sat wearing a three-piece suit and holding a gold pocket watch.

"Hello, hello!" the man said, rising from the desk. "Is this him? Is this *the one*?"

An Impressive Discovery

"I don't believe it!" Charlie exclaimed, popping his knuckles. Wisdom's message was waiting for him after dinner. Charlie had written to him on a number of occasions, but this was the first time Wisdom Willows had ever replied.

Charlie,

Your book discovery is quite impressive. Where did you find it? Who wrote it? You said the book caused your EMF detector to go crazy? Explain. Books don't usually register readings on EMF detectors. I'm interested in learning more, and I'm excited that you chose to contact me.

Sincerely,
WW

"*Wisdom Willows*," Charlie whispered reverently. "Writing to *me*!"

After several attempts to sound official, Charlie typed his answer on the keyboard, settling for relaying every detail of his discovery.

Then, Charlie hurriedly changed into pajamas and sat down on his bed with the heavy book centered in his lap. From what he had seen, there were no legible numbers or words on any of the pages, but maybe a second look would spark a discovery.

At some point before nine o'clock, and after he had been searching for over an hour, Charlie noticed the curtain fluttering out of the corner of his eye. Sitting up, he yawned and blinked. The window was closed, and no air pumped through the apartment's vents, but there had been definite movement. Charlie's skin prickled, and an uncomfortable pit began to form in his stomach.

"Stop wasting time," he whispered to himself. He couldn't read the words in the book, but maybe he could pick up on some sort of pattern or recognize a symbol from his research. He stared down at the opened pages once more and honed his focus.

Instincts

The screech of chair legs scooting across the floor echoed through the office as the man in the three-piece suit stood up. He rounded the desk and grasped Walter's hand before Walter could think twice about it.

"Here you are, my boy. My dear, dear boy." His eyes twinkled as he shook Walter's hand vigorously. "Very good, Frederick. You may return to your duties."

The man with the clipboard nodded. "Yes, sir."

Walter watched Frederick leave and wondered how he might retrieve his hand without coming across as rude. When shaking a hand, one had to let go after three pumps, five at the most. Walter knew that. Everyone knew that. But the man with the pocket watch didn't seem to have grasped the concept. His hand felt moist and smooth, as though he used too much lotion. Did dead people need lotion? Walter began to wonder how he could feel things at all. Wasn't he a spirit? Didn't that complicate one's ability to feel things?

"The name's Darwin Pollock, and I am the Head Assigner of Agents for HLTA at the Afterlife Academy." He relinquished his hold on Walter's fingers, and Walter jammed them into his pocket to prevent another handshake.

"HL what?" Walter questioned.

Darwin blinked. "HLTA. Stands for High-Level Target Assignments. It gives meaning to our establishment. The whole Afterlife Academy works because of HLTA, and every assignment must be stamped and approved at this desk." He patted the tabletop. "By me."

"Cool." Walter glanced sideways at the lion statue and whistled. "Where did you get that?"

Darwin's smile dimmed momentarily as he followed Walter's gaze. "You don't know why you're here, do you?" Darwin asked. "Frederick didn't tell you?"

Walter made a face as if he'd just eaten something and couldn't tell whether or not it contained raisins.

"You registered a perfect score. One hundred percent!" Darwin exclaimed. "Not in the three hundred years I've worked here has anyone done that."

"Really?" Walter tugged at his collar. "A perfect score?"

Darwin nodded vigorously.

"On what?"

"On your entry exam, of course! No one scores one hundred percent on that questionnaire. It's unheard of. Do you know what that means?"

Walter thought back to the lengthy list of questions Alton had given him in the Categorizing Office. Questions concerning his life. Ones about bumper stickers and meals he had ordered at fast food restaurants with his family.

Questions about what he wore on picture day in the fourth grade. Pointless questions. Multiple-choice questions with no right answer to choose from. He had skimmed most of them and circled randomly without considering what they asked.

"Um . . . wow." Walter scratched his head in confusion. "Does it mean I can stay?"

Darwin's lower lip curled out and he snorted. "Stay? Can you stay?" He belly laughed and sat down on the edge of the desk. "My boy, you're exactly what the Academy needs. Instinctual. Aggressive. A take-the-bull-by-the-horns type of Agent."

The queasiness in Walter's stomach vanished.

"But I'm not going to let you stay," Darwin added, and Walter's hopes plummeted.

"Why not?" How could earning a perfect score on the questionnaire get him kicked out of the Academy? Unless . . . "I didn't cheat, if that's what you mean! I just—"

"I know you didn't cheat, son. No one can cheat on Alton's exams. He personally observes and stamps each one to assure their authenticity. And to be honest, he's the only one who really understands them."

"Then why am I in trouble?"

"You're not in any trouble." Darwin interlocked his fingers and pressed them against his lips. "You are the future. A shining star. Someone destined for greatness. Walter, I am so pleased, so very, very pleased that you opted to join the Academy! It gives me hope."

Walter grinned awkwardly. "So . . . I *can* stay?" He was getting confused.

Darwin reached out and placed his hands firmly on Walter's shoulders. "On the contrary, you've already been assigned." Darwin returned to his chair and scooted up to the desk.

Perhaps Walter hadn't understood the meaning of the word "assigned." He wanted to sit down, but the closest available chair rested in the corner next to a large potted fern. Instead, he leaned forward and gripped the edge of the desk for support. Darwin opened a drawer and pulled out a laminated card similar to the ones the Logan boys had shown Walter earlier.

"Here's your HLT, though that's what we call every one of them, no matter how minor or insignificant. High-Level. It's standard. You'll understand after a few days in the field. The particulars are listed on the reverse." He flipped the card over and ran his index finger down the fine print.

Darwin might as well have been speaking in guinea pig.

"I'm going down?" The latter part of the sentence squeaked out of Walter's trembling lips. Was this good news? Walter sniffed, then swallowed. It sounded like good news. Maybe he would see the Logan brothers. They could hang out. Have some fun. Until some demon ate him. It didn't take a genius to understand the importance of training. "I think you've made a mistake. I don't know what I'm doing. I need training!"

"You don't need training. You're a natural. The test proves it. Alton knows what he's doing with those tests. He's never been wrong before, and I don't think he ever will be."

Okay. Time to come clean.

"Look, I just made that stuff up. I didn't even read the

questions." Typically in school, when a teacher praised him for performing exceptionally well on a test, a feat Walter rarely accomplished, he knew better than to tell the truth. Never tell them you made stuff up. But this felt different.

"Instinct," Darwin whispered. "You used your instinct. You know, you remind me of me when I first joined the Academy. Oh, I tried to show humility when they told me about my near-perfect score. But deep down inside, in here"—Darwin pressed his fingers into his stomach—"I knew it to be true."

"You got a perfect score on your exam too?"

"A *near*-perfect score. I only missed two. And, in three hundred years, no one else has even come close. Perhaps you and I are linked somehow." Darwin paused, musing, then snapped back to business. "At any rate, these are dangerous times, Walter Prairie, and training would be a waste of valuable resources. Trust me, you'll do wonderfully!" He slid the laminated card across the desk to Walter's reluctant fingers.

Walter glanced over the card and stared at a bright-orange boy. Orange hair. Orange freckles. An annoyingly toothy smile.

"'Charlie Dewdle,'" he read aloud. "Why's he important?"

Darwin leaned forward and pointed to the information on the back of the card. "Age, closest relatives, likes, dislikes, sleep patterns, fears, et cetera." Walter flipped the card over and perused the information. "Everything you need to know is on the card."

"So what happens when I need to do some spell or something like that? How do I do it?" Walter asked.

"Here." Darwin pressed something else into Walter's hand. "This is a ready-reference pamphlet. It lists the basics every Afterlife Agent should know. Now Walter, listen to me closely. You've been selected for a covert assignment. Do you understand what that means?"

"Not a clue."

Darwin's eyes sparkled. "This is an observation mission. We don't really know all the details of what's going on. It's up to you to investigate. It's highly unlikely you'll need any of this"—he tapped the pamphlet—"but if you do, follow your instincts."

Walter took a deep breath. The poor guy really believed in him.

"Come. You may use my personal passageway." Darwin held out a hand toward the door behind his desk.

Walter shrugged, took a last look at his sudden and enthusiastic mentor, and exited the room.

How would he know when his instinct was necessary? Would it just come naturally to him like the questionnaire? Well, maybe his first assignment would be nothing more than a babysitting job with the orange-headed goof.

That, he could handle.

The Summoner's Handbook

Charlie had been flipping through the book for hours. He still couldn't make any sense of it.

Meanwhile, and unbeknownst to Charlie, he had become quite popular among the creatures of the Underworld. His bedroom buzzed with excitement. Shades crowded around the mattress, scrambling over one another to steal a peek at the book. Others hovered shoulder to shoulder over his bed, snarling, gnashing, and groaning in anticipation.

"*The Summoner's Handbook!*" one shade whispered.

"How can it be?" questioned another, flitting around near the ceiling of Charlie's bedroom.

Had this boy really found it? If so, surely they would be rewarded for bringing it to their master. But they had to make sure it was indeed the book. Raising a false alarm would be a painful mistake.

"Could—" one shade started to say, hesitating as if not

wanting to sound foolish in front of the others. "Could *we* make it work?"

A unified murmuring began among the growing number of shades. They had all heard stories of *The Summoner's Handbook*, of course. But deciphering its codes, reading extensive, complex passages, opening gateways . . . those sorts of things didn't exactly fit under their job descriptions. Shades were merely wanderers. Spies. Operating the book required a more qualified being.

Three more shades spiraled into the room. "The master has spoken!" they shouted together. "We must act immediately! We must call . . . *her!*"

The murmuring ceased, and Charlie's room grew quiet. Forming a circle, the shades linked their arms, bowed their cloaked heads, and began to chant.

The temperature in the room plummeted.

II

Battle With a Banshee

Walter heard a slurping sound, as if a dentist were suctioning saliva out of his mouth. A force yanked his body through the door in Darwin's office, and he plunged through a blindingly white column of light. Before he had time to scream, he was standing in a closet. There were shoe boxes on the floor and a hamper of dirty clothing next to him. Walter took a moment to control his breathing, and then peered through the slats in the closet door.

It looked like someone had hung about fifty graduation robes to dry on a clothesline. What were they doing hanging up in a bedroom? Then Walter realized that the robes were moving and had faces. Tall, ghastly creatures with red eyes, quivering mouths, and dark, bony fingers hovered in a circle around the room. All of them were focused on the redheaded boy shivering on the bed.

"Dude, get out of here!" Walter shouted at his HLT as he burst out of the closet.

Charlie didn't acknowledge Walter, but the shades let out a collective squeal. Several floating closest to Walter swarmed nearer, zapping him with electric energy from their fingertips.

"That stings!" yelled Walter.

"Do *not* interfere!" one of the creatures hissed.

"Begone!" said another.

Walter quickly backed into the closet and held up his hands to surrender. "Okay, take it easy."

The creatures withdrew and rejoined the circle.

Frosted breath plumed from Charlie's lips. He was wearing pajamas and appeared to be reading a book, completely unaware of the atrocity happening all around him.

Did this sort of thing happen all the time during the first day on the job? Walter poked his head slightly out of the closet. Maybe he would find another kid from the Academy surveying the crime scene. Maybe this was just a training session. Maybe Walter was in the wrong room.

But there was no one else. And no way for him to get back to Darwin's office. Walter had forgotten to ask for one of those little white clips that would allow him to get back to the Academy. He was stuck. Walter pressed his hand against the wall. It passed right through. The sensation tingled in his fingertips. He didn't mind it after a few moments, but he gaped openmouthed at his vanishing hand nonetheless.

"No way!" Could he also float and fly like those black robes in the bedroom? Concentrating on an image of himself drifting up toward the ceiling, Walter closed his eyes and tried to fly. Nothing happened. Behind him, several of the creatures cackled, bringing him back into reality. He watched them swirling around Charlie. What was he supposed to do? There were so many of them, and their fingers hurt.

"I'll go get help!" Walter whispered, even though Charlie couldn't hear him. He strode forward and approached the rear of the closet. He'd entered from there. Maybe if he stepped back through that same wall, he'd end up in Darwin's office. Walter closed his eyes and immediately started giggling. Passing through walls tickled in the worst sort of way.

When he stopped giggling, he had exited to the other side of the wall. But instead of seeing Darwin and that enormous lion statue, Walter found a little girl in pigtails standing in front of a bathroom mirror, brushing her teeth and gargling as she sang.

The girl spat into the sink, stuck out her tongue at her reflection, and said, "Die, sugar bugs, die!"

"Hey, little girl, where's Darwin?" Walter asked.

The girl sucked her toothbrush dry and chomped her teeth together. She did not notice Walter.

Deciding to take a more drastic approach, Walter reached for the girl's arm, but his hand passed effortlessly through her, as it had done with the wall.

"Mom!" the girl shouted at the bathroom door. "Charlie left his towel on the floor, and his dirty underwear, too!" From somewhere else in the house came a woman's muffled response. Then the girl started slurping water from the running faucet.

Obviously, Walter was invisible to human beings, including little pigtailed girls.

Walter threw his hands in the air. "This is stupid! Darwin, can you hear me?"

Silence.

"Look, about that exam—I just made it all up!"

Nothing.

He ran back to Charlie's bedroom. The chanting had grown to a thunderous level. The room, which had been overly crowded before, now swarmed with more dark spirits. Even though light poured from Charlie's bedside lamp, Walter could hardly see his target in the midst of the swirling black masses. The boy had slumped over and was twitching and seizing in rhythm with their chanting. A large form started taking shape near the ceiling above Charlie's bed. The object dwarfed the other spirits and became less distorted as the chanting grew louder. Tentacles stretched from what looked like a grotesque woman dressed all in black. Her hair stood on end as if electrified, and her bulbous white eyes protruded from their sockets.

"That can't be good!" Why was Charlie Dewdle just lying there, slumped over like a moron? Any reasonable kid would've left by now. Couldn't he sense something terrible was about to happen? There were too many creatures for Walter to fight, and how would he even do that in the first place? His pulse quickened. He couldn't fail his assignment within the first hour.

Walter jabbed his hand in his pocket and pulled out the ready-reference pamphlet. Five folded pages with large boldface type, a couple of pictures of Guardian Agents in various poses, and a few step-by-step bullet points of instruction were all he found.

"This is it?" He pored over the pamphlet ravenously, sheer panic overwhelming him.

STEP 1—ASSESS THE SITUATION. Agents should never act until they have properly assessed the level of danger. A calm demeanor will . . .

Yeah, whatever! There was no need to stop and assess the level of danger. There was no doubt—it was bad. He skipped to Step 2.

STEP 2—IDENTIFY THE ENEMY. Agents should know the makeup and constitution of each level of dark creature, from the basic Underworld nuisance to the most threatening demon.

Walter looked at the accompanying pictures as he read.

Consider this on a four-point scale, with one being the easiest enemy to engage and four being the deadliest.

LEVEL 1—SHADES. Composed of wispy, dark material and generally characterized by their high-pitched squealing and whimsical flight patterns, shades pose the lowest threat to Agents. Avoid attacking them in groups of five or more and be wary of their touch, which, although causing no permanent threat or harm, can induce a slightly uncomfortable jarring sensation.

Walter's eyes shot up from the book as he remembered what was more than a slightly uncomfortable sensation when the shades had zapped him.

"Right. Shades." His eyes darted around the room. "More than five. Definitely more than five! What happens when there's more than five? Darwin, you've got to hear me!"

The giant creature floating above the bed had grown more distinct. The chanting continued from the shades, and the monster's eyes homed in on their target. If Walter failed to act, Charlie didn't stand a chance. Walter looked back down at the pamphlet.

> LEVEL 2—WRAITHS. Humanoid in shape and characterized by bloodred cloaks and scythelike claws, wraiths make formidable opponents. Avoid staring directly into their eyes, as this will inflict immediate paralysis, and do not, under any circumstances . . .

"Blah, blah, blah!" Walter scanned the room. No wraiths yet, so no need to dwell on them. What he needed to know was the level of the hideous floating woman in the center of the room. The one almost completely formed into an evil octopus lady.

> LEVEL 3—DARK OMENS. Like wraiths, Dark Omens are humanoid in shape. Despite having several extra tentacle-like appendages, they are entirely female in appearance. Primarily used as harbingers of death and frequently referred to as banshees, or miseries,

> Dark Omens always pose an immediate threat to the life of an Agent's HLT (High-Level Target). Dark Omens are the only creatures capable of transporting living humans directly to the Underworld against their will.

Walter reread that line. Transporting living humans to the Underworld? That didn't sound fun.

> Unpredictable and deadly, Dark Omens use their unnatural abilities only on rare occasions. Refrain from direct confrontation, as their voices are capable of shattering spiritual bones. Never engage alone . . .

> LEVEL 4—DEMONS. Demons are the rulers of the Underworld and control Levels 1 to 3. They themselves have a variety of classifications, from lesser to . . .

Walter didn't need to read any further. There were no demons in the room, from what he could see, but this was not going to be easy. If he didn't think of some sort of plan of action, Walter's HLT would be transported to the Underworld by Old Ugly.

"Come on, Walter. The head of the Afterlife Academy believes you can do this. You can do this."

The chanting came to a chilling conclusion, and the banshee was now fully formed. One of its spectral tentacles drifted down and grazed Charlie's cheek. Charlie writhed and began to convulse.

Walter took several quick breaths and readied himself to do something totally insane.

"Hey, losers! Why don't you pick on someone your own size?"

The outburst startled the shades. Snarling, they surrounded Walter.

"Begone! Do not interfere! We shall attack!" Their voices hissed like the sound of air leaking from a tire.

Walter had a respectable record when it came to after-school fights. He had no clue if his hands would pass right through the shades like everything else, but it was worth a shot. He swung his right fist and connected with the midsection of the closest shade. He felt an electric bolt go up his arm, but like a black towel in a dryer, the shade tumbled, releasing an agonizing cry. Walter stared at the creature. He could hurt the shades! He snapped his eyes toward the others.

"Leave well enough alone!" a voice called from somewhere in the middle of the crowd. "Do not interfere!"

"Yeah, you said that already." Walter flexed his fingers in and out of a balled fist. "Now get out of my way, or I'll thump every one of you!" He brought both hands up, squaring off like a boxer. To his surprise, the shades retreated a few paces.

One of them extended its arm to shock him, but Walter reacted with a right hook to the creature's hooded skull. Squeals erupted. Walter felt his jaw chatter from the electricity passing through him, but he was causing more damage to the shades than they were to him.

"Want some more?" He made a few sparring jabs. Their cloaks flapped. Their eyes narrowed. Yet they seemed to fear him.

Undeterred, the banshee wrapped a tentacle around Charlie's throat and into the unconscious boy's mouth.

"Back off, ugly!" Walter shouted. The banshee paid him no attention, alert only to its prey. Walter highly doubted his uppercuts would have the same effect on the wriggling Dark Omen. Should he hop on top of it? Wrestle it? Maybe take jabs at its eyes with his fingers?

The tentacle slithered deeper into Charlie's throat. Walter didn't have time to check his pamphlet, but he guessed a banshee's tentacle in anyone's mouth was not a good idea. Walter raced toward the banshee.

The surrounding shades attacked, zapping him from all sides with electricity. Fifty different strikes hit him in the chest, the back, and the head. His vision blurred. His knees felt gooey. Walter punched, kicked, and head-butted his way through the swarm. The shades weren't happy with their injuries, but Walter was losing. And so was Charlie. Three more tentacles had entered Charlie's mouth.

Walter made one final charge, propelling himself through the air with the last of his energy. He fell through the banshee and collapsed flat on top of Charlie.

The Beginning of an Unusual Friendship

Charlie opened his eyes and blinked as torrential rain peppered his bedroom window.

"Yuck!" He gagged and stuck out his tongue. He had eaten part of a dead toad once. Not his idea, of course. Grady Hinkens had forced him to eat it in third grade. This tasted worse.

Charlie pawed at his eyes with his palms, wondering if he had fallen asleep in a coat closet. What was with all the cloaks hanging everywhere?

Several pairs of eyes peered out from the cloaks, and Charlie sucked in a breath. Moving fabric flapped about him, as if blown by a strong wind. Above him, floating near his ceiling, an ugly woman gaped, openmouthed.

Charlie could smell sulfurous brimstone, even taste the pungent flavors on his tongue. His skin felt cold, and everything around him seemed in perfect focus. All of his senses seemed to be functioning properly. What kind of dream could do that?

"Don't just sit there, doofus, get out of here." A boy's voice, loud and piercing, sounded in Charlie's ears.

"What?" Charlie exclaimed, spinning around in search of the source of the voice. "Who said that?"

"You can hear me?"

"Yes, I can hear you!" Charlie's heart leapt into his throat as the woman above him released a shuddering scream and then rapidly dissolved into the ceiling. The cloaks circled around him, glaring with evil red eyes and squealing like baby pigs. They were not pieces of clothing at all. Charlie remembered seeing something like them in his books on paranormal creatures.

Shades!

What were shades doing in his room?

But as soon as he noticed them, they vanished. Charlie clutched his hand to his chest. He collapsed backward onto his pillow. The rain on the window settled until only a few sporadic drops kissed the glass. "Mom's fried okra and those onions," he babbled. "They always give me bad dreams. Get a grip, Charlie."

"That wasn't a dream," the boy's voice said.

Charlie jerkily sat up. "Is this some kind of prank? Real funny."

"It's not a prank. How can you hear me?" the boy asked.

"With my ears. I'm not deaf. Where are you hiding?" Charlie dropped to the floor and snapped the cover up to peer under his bed. He pushed around a few boxes of old toys but found no one under there. Racing toward the closet, he kicked the T-shirts aside, ready to scream for his parents if anyone appeared. But the closet stood empty as well. He must be losing his mind. Charlie sat down on his bed, removed his socks, and yawned as he fluffed his pillow.

"You're not going to sleep, are you?" the boy's voice asked. "Not after all that."

Charlie flung himself at his bedroom door, wrenching it open.

"Aha!" He stared out into an empty hallway. His shoulders slumped in surrender. "I give up. Please come out and show yourself."

The boy began to laugh. But the laughter sounded bewildered rather than scathing. "I didn't think anyone living could hear me."

"Well, congratulations," Charlie said. "I guess I'm the lucky— Wait. What do you mean, 'anyone *living*'?" The voice chuckled, and the tiny red hairs on the back of Charlie's neck prickled. "That's it. I'm getting my dad."

"At this hour?"

It was dark out, but Charlie couldn't remember getting ready for bed or kissing his mom goodnight. He glanced at the hall clock. Just after midnight. His dad had to wake up early every morning for work and wouldn't appreciate having his sleep interrupted. But what choice did Charlie have?

"What are you going to tell him? That you're hearing voices?" the voice chattered right behind Charlie's ear, and he whirled to face the intruder. Only his reflection peered back at him from the hallway mirror.

"This isn't funny. I don't want to play this game anymore." His eyes darted left to right and even shot up, as if expecting to see someone hanging from the light fixture.

"Look, dude, you're not going to believe this, but I'm standing . . . inside you."

Out of Control

"You're *what?*" Charlie's lips pulled into an uncomfortable grin. He felt nauseated. Okra and onions always did that to him, but this felt different. Not wasting any time, Charlie hurried down the hallway, but he hesitated before knocking on his parents' bedroom door.

"I'm not playing any games," the boy's voice said calmly. "My name's Walter Prairie, and I'm a spirit, and I'm inside you."

A pasty gob of saliva slid down Charlie's throat as he swallowed. The doorknob, though less than a finger's width from him, seemed a mile away. Shades, a creepy floating woman, and spirit visitations? What had Charlie gotten himself into?

"Okay, let's say I believe you. What kind of spirit are you?"

"Uh, I'm a dead one. Duh."

Charlie blinked. He could hear the murmuring snores

of his parents just beyond the door. "Are you some sort of warning spirit, like a . . . Are you my conscience?"

"Like Pinocchio and Jiminy Cricket?" Walter laughed. "I don't think so, man."

"Okay. You're not my conscience. But only I can hear you?"

"I think so," Walter said. "But let's test it out, just to make sure."

"How are you going to—"

"*Wake up, losers!!!*" Walter's voice boomed in Charlie's ears.

Charlie held his breath and stared at his parents' bedroom door, listening for any movement. The shouting should've sent them crashing out of bed.

"See? It probably has something to do with me being inside you. I don't know for sure. So, where do you go to school?" Walter took on a casual tone.

Charlie once more considered waking his parents but then thought about his dad's reaction. Voices in his head . . . His room swarming with shades . . . He'd be grounded for sure. "Cunningham Middle School," he answered. "Why?"

"Are there any cute girls at Cunningham?"

"I'm sorry, is that really important right now?" Charlie tiptoed back to his bedroom and closed the door with a soft click.

"Girls are always important. At my school, Yorkshire Middle, there are tons of cute girls." Walter sounded more like a buddy at a sleepover than a ghost. But Charlie didn't have buddies, and he didn't have sleepovers, so he was only guessing.

The top drawer of Charlie's bedside table held a stack of magazines containing pictures of zombies and vampires. As Walter rambled on, Charlie went to get one and flipped through until he found the article he was looking for. Holding up his hand with his pointer and middle fingers curled downward in hexing position, he suddenly shouted, "Demon, begone!"

Silence.

Charlie puffed out his cheeks in relief.

"What was that supposed to do?" Walter asked.

Charlie jumped. "It was supposed to get rid of you," he said with a groan.

"Get rid of me? I'm not a demon!" Walter's voice rose in anger. "I'm an Afterlife Academy Agent, and I've been sent here to protect you."

"I've never heard of the Afterlife Academy, and why do I need protecting?" Charlie tossed the magazine on the floor.

"Did you not see what was going on in your room? Lucky I showed up when I did."

Charlie pounded his hands against his head. "Please stop talking for a second, and let me think." He needed to find a more peaceful location, one where he could gather his thoughts.

Charlie walked to the study and opened the door.

"What's with all the birds?" Walter asked.

Ignoring him, Charlie poked his finger through the wires, allowing the small creatures to nibble. He always found refuge among his feathered friends. Their soft fluttering and chirping soothed his mind after a troubling day at school.

"If you're telling the truth, there has to be a logical reason for why you were sent to me. And why those things tried to attack me." Charlie stroked the head of one of his finches. "For starters, it's obvious the cloaked black creatures were—"

"Wraiths!" Walter blurted out.

Charlie shook his head. "No. Not wraiths. Wraiths are much bigger and more dangerous. Those were shades. Wraiths can't enter homes—not without an invitation." He rattled off a memorized definition from one of his magazines. "Shades are nothing more than minions of more powerful creatures like demons. And all Underworld creatures are subject to the law of demons."

"And you know this . . . how?" Walter asked.

"I read books and magazines." Charlie had devoted most of his young life to the study of paranormal creatures. His extensive collection of literature had proven its value. "But I don't have a clue what that other thing was. That woman." Whatever it was, it was powerful.

"It's a banshee," Walter said.

Charlie smiled dismissively. "Don't be stupid. You have no idea what you're talking about. Banshees don't exist. That's just what people in places like Ireland believe."

"Whatever. It was a banshee. That much I do know. My pamphlet called it a Dark Omen. And I think I know more than you on the subject. I am an Afterlife Agent, and your Guardian Agent, after all."

"Fine. We'll call it a banshee until I can discover its real title. What's this pamphlet you keep talking about?" Charlie checked the level of the canaries' water container by tapping the bottle with his finger. A few drops fell to the bottom.

"It's a ready-reference pamphlet for Afterlife Agents like myself."

"I'm going to need to see it," Charlie said. "Maybe it can help us figure things out."

Charlie heard Walter grunting and straining. "Uh, I can't reach it. I'm kinda stuck inside you at the moment."

"Then why don't you get out?"

"Believe me, I've been trying to do that for a while now," Walter said.

With his birds sufficiently fed, Charlie sat down in the desk chair. He connected to the Internet and then wiggled his fingers above the keyboard.

"Hey!" Walter said suddenly.

Charlie yelped. "Would you stop scaring me?"

"What am I supposed to do if I want to talk?"

"Try saying things calmly. Like in a whisper."

"Can you check something for me on the computer?" Walter whispered using a very creepy voice. Charlie's skin turned cold from the sound of it, but at least the spirit had taken his advice.

Within a couple of minutes, per Walter's request, Charlie brought up the online site of the *Poleman County Times*, the main newspaper of Walter's hometown in Virginia. An article about a tragic lightning storm accident appeared on the screen.

"You were struck by lightning?" Charlie asked in a solemn tone once he finished the article.

"Yeah. Bummer, huh?"

"That was just a few days ago. Then you came directly here?"

"Well, not exactly. First I went to a Categorizing Office. Then I was supposed to go through four years of training at the Afterlife Academy before I got assigned to someone. But"—Walter sighed—"I'm a bit of a natural."

"What does that even mean?" Charlie hovered the cursor over the black-and-white school photo of Walter Prairie, a tough-looking kid with a confident smile and what looked like either a cold sore or a cut on his lower lip. The chances of the two of them hanging out in a normal situation seemed highly unlikely. Of all the spirits to be possessed by, why did Charlie have to have someone like Walter?

"It means I have a knack for this type of stuff even if I don't know what I'm doing in the beginning. I just have to use my instincts."

"So you don't have any training?" Charlie asked.

"Nope."

"Perfect." Charlie didn't believe in relying wholly on instincts. And he seemed to know more than Walter did. If the shades came back, how was Walter going to help him at all? Charlie navigated to SpiritSpy.org and typed "spirit possession" into the search bar.

Several images flashed on the screen, all of them displaying people either sleeping or sitting in chairs with their eyes closed while faded representations of ghosts hovered above them. After reading a few paragraphs, Charlie clicked on one of the video links.

Black-and-white and laced with static, video footage of a

supposed spirit possession blipped on the monitor. The date in the bottom right corner of the screen had been blurred out deliberately. A boy waist-deep under his sheets writhed in his bed as several adult onlookers circled him. Charlie turned up the audio as a man's voice chanted through the computer speakers. It was shoddy work. Poor lighting and sound. Not one close-up of the boy in the bed. He was the main attraction, for crying out loud!

Charlie snickered. "Who filmed this? It's so fake!"

"Turn that junk off," Walter whispered.

Charlie leaned closer to the screen. "The guy can't even hold the camera still."

"Did you hear me?" Walter's voice rose shakily. "I said, turn it off!"

"I heard you," Charlie answered. "But I'm not finished watching. Ah, come on! That boy's not even acting believable. He keeps looking at the camera! Amateurs."

"I don't care. It's freaking me out!"

"Who ever heard of a ghost being scared of other ghosts? Who are you, Casper?" Charlie sighed. "We're going to have to find a better instructional video. This one's worthless."

Suddenly, Charlie's hand yanked forward out of his control, clicked the mouse, and X'ed out of the video. As if sensing the disruption, all seven birds, including Doris the parakeet, erupted with a cacophony of unsettling squawks.

"How—how did you do that?" Charlie blubbered, flexing his fingers.

"I *told* you to turn it off. I don't like watching weird ghost videos. And I don't know how I did that. I'm trying to do it right now, but I can't."

"Well, please don't." Charlie scooted his chair back from the computer.

"Charlie," an eerie woman's voice whispered from the doorway.

Charlie and Walter screamed at the top of their lungs in harmony.

Lack of Sleep

The birds joined in as the boys' screams echoed through the small apartment like screeching tires at a demolition derby.

Charlie's mother stood in the doorway wearing a nightgown, arms folded in front of her. "Do you realize what time it is? You're going to wake your father!"

"Too late," Charlie's dad muttered from the hallway.

"What have we told you about playing on the computer after bedtime?" she asked.

"But, Mom, this is different," Charlie tried to reason. "I was just—"

"Don't tell her anything about me, stupid," Walter said in Charlie's ears.

"Shut up!" Charlie snapped.

His mom's jaw dropped, and his dad's stern face appeared in the doorway. "You do *not* talk to your mother like that!"

Charlie put his hands up in submission and backpedaled. "Oh no, I wasn't talking to her. I was talking to—"

"Watch it," Walter warned. "I don't think you should be telling them about me just yet."

Closing his eyes, Charlie swallowed. "I was talking to my birds. They were about to get noisy again, and I know how much you hate that when you're trying to sleep."

That got him off the hook for snapping at his mother, but he was still banished from the computer for the rest of the week—with the threat of much worse if he didn't go to bed immediately.

"Man, you got off easy," Walter said, once Charlie had nestled down under his covers.

"Easy? We just lost our ability to research what's going on," Charlie whispered. "Thanks a lot!"

"So? It's only for two days. What about your cell phone? Don't you have Internet?"

"I don't have a cell phone."

"What? How old are you? Everyone in middle school has a cell phone."

"Would you please stop shouting? I can hear everything you say." Charlie rubbed his eyes and yawned. None of this made sense. Where had Walter come from? Why had he possessed Charlie? And most important, when was he going to leave?

"Hey!" Walter shouted once more. "Oh, sorry." He lowered his voice. "What does your dad do for a living?"

"My dad? What does it matter?"

"I just remembered something important. Demons and

other Underworld creatures are attracted to kids because of their parents' jobs."

Charlie sat up and rested against the headboard. "Did you make that up just now? That's really worthless information."

"It's not worthless," Walter protested. "Just answer the question."

"He drives an armored car." Charlie dropped back down onto his pillow.

"Like a tank?"

"What? No! An armored car. He picks up money from businesses and delivers it to the bank."

"Is it dangerous?"

"I guess. He has to carry a gun."

"Maybe that's it! Does he have to shoot people from time to time?" Walter probed.

"Seriously, would you please just be quiet for a few hours? I need to get my sleep. It's the only way I'll have a clear head tomorrow so we can figure out how to get rid of you."

Walter didn't argue. Charlie rolled over and tried his hardest to fall asleep—a task made extremely difficult when Walter turned out to be a heavy breather.

Hoonga's Assignment

Down in the Underworld, an enormous demon named Hoonga sat behind a stone desk. Around him, dusty chairs lay overturned. Mangled pieces of garbage floated on the backs of insects. Dark sludge bubbled from a gaping crack in a refrigerator and pooled on the floor next to a rolled-up rug. Occasionally the rug would twitch as something caught within the rolls released a low whimper.

It was Hoonga's office, and it was just the way he liked it.

Hoonga was a hideous sight to behold. He had brown, leathery skin, elephant-like tusks, and a single blinking eyeball centered on his forehead. He owned the title of Controller at a highly successful demon outpost. As of late, his business had been booming. This wasn't the case with other demon outposts, and Hoonga felt incredibly fortunate. Almost all of his staff had been called upon to carry out multiple tasks, ranging from temptations to full-fledged human possessions. All he had to do was sit around and wait for his demons to finish their assignments and report back to him as the riches from a variety of benefactors flowed continuously into his office.

The demon examined a colored photograph in front of him and drummed his black claws against his chin. "This is him?" Hoonga asked the lesser demon seated cross-legged on the corner of the desk. "You're sure this is his picture?"

Trutti's floppy bat ears shook as he vigorously nodded his head. "Yes, master. The shades assured me this is the one you're looking for."

Hoonga lifted the photograph off the desk and squinted his single eye. "Doesn't look like much, does he?"

Trutti shook his head. "He seems like an easily squashable child to me."

Hoonga raised his eyebrow and smirked. "And yet he has somehow acquired the most powerful book in the Underworld and bested a fully formed banshee. Not to mention a whole squadron of shades."

Trutti discovered an annoying itch on the back of his neck and immediately went to work at it. "He didn't do that alone, master. He had the help of his Agent."

"His Agent," Hoonga muttered under his breath. "That's what bothers me."

"You know what you should do?" Trutti snapped his fingers. "You should send some hired muscle. Someone to get the job done. The shades can be so unreliable."

Hoonga began to nod in agreement, but then he narrowed his eye and glared at Trutti. "Are you trying to tell me how to run my post?"

"Oh no! Never!" Trutti bowed his head low. "I was merely making a suggestion, I would never dream of—"

Hoonga held up a finger to cut Trutti off, and the lesser demon instantly fell silent. The Cyclops pondered his options and then pressed the call button on the intercom.

"Yes?" a sniveling voice asked above the static of the receiver.

"Send word to Gorge," Hoonga instructed. "Tell him to come to my office at once. I'm in need of his services."

"Of course, master," the voice responded.

Hoonga tossed the photograph aside and heaved himself up from his chair. Trutti stood as well, but even standing upon the desk, the tiny creature was dwarfed by Hoonga's massive frame.

"Excellent choice, master," Trutti squeaked. "Gorge is a frightening spectacle."

"He's an idiot," Hoonga said. "But he's a powerful idiot. And if what you say is true"—once more, he raised the photo of the boy for a closer look—"Gorge should be just enough muscle to capture this easily squashable child."

16

Mo Makes His Mark

Charlie had a horrible night's sleep. There had been actual shades in his bedroom! Things Charlie had only read about in his magazines were now happening to him. But that wasn't the worst of it. For a dead guy, Walter sure had a lot of things on his mind. After only about an hour of silence, save for his breathing, he didn't stop talking until early in the morning. Before Charlie knew it, the blaring shrill of his alarm woke him up for the day.

"So, let's get started," Walter said, once Charlie had sat up and stretched. "What exactly were you doing last night? Before I showed up?"

"What do you mean? I was sleeping."

"No you weren't. Were you playing with a Ouija board or something?"

Charlie rolled his eyes. "I was just in my room. I got ready for bed and started looking at— Oh my gosh!" He stared at the object lying on the floor next to his bed. "The book!"

"What book?"

"I found some weird book buried behind the shopping mall yesterday. I was looking at it after dinner when all this started."

"Do you still have it?" Walter's voice grew louder.

"Yeah, it's"—he gulped and pointed to the floor, where the old leather book rested beneath a pair of his dirty socks and a few of his magazines—"right there. It must've fallen off the bed during the, you know, the whole shade . . . thing."

"It just looks like some dumb book."

"It's not dumb. But Wisdom Willows said that books don't generally register readings on EMF detectors, so I—"

"Wait a minute," Walter interrupted. "Who said that? And what the heck is an EMF detector?"

"Wisdom Willows," Charlie answered in an exhausted tone. "He's a genius. He runs SpiritSpy.org and is the author of fifteen books on paranormal activity. I've read them all. Wisdom gives talks all over the country. And an EMF detector collects paranormal data and points out hot spots where there are spirits."

"Uh-huh." Walter didn't seem to be absorbing all of this.

"Anyways, when I found the book, the EMF detector started blipping and stuff, and I figured maybe it contained paranormal signatures." Charlie was rattling off the information at a rapid speed, his voice energized. "But then Wisdom said he didn't think books could register data on an EMF—"

"How is any of this useful?" Walter snapped.

Charlie's chest heaved. "How come you didn't notice the book? Didn't you see me reading it?"

"Oh, right. Your room is filled with dozens of shades and one fat octopus lady, and you expect me to figure out that some book has to do with it?"

"Well, you're *supposed* to know how to protect me," Charlie said.

"Hey! I think I'm doing a pretty good job so far. You're not dead . . . yet."

Charlie swung his feet over the edge of the bed. But when he saw the book still lying there, he decided to drop to the floor on the other side.

"I've gotta get online and do some more research. Someone will know what kind of book that is."

"Well, hurry up and go!" Walter urged.

Charlie reached for the doorknob, but then stopped and groaned. "I can't. My parents forbade me to use the computer, remember?"

"So just sneak in there. No one's gonna know, and what they don't know can't hurt them."

"Believe me, they'll know. My birds are always super noisy just before breakfast." Charlie hurriedly changed out of his pajamas and into school clothes. "It's okay. I have computer lab right after lunch." He picked the mysterious book up off the floor and hid it under his pillow.

"You're not going to take it with us?" Walter asked.

"I don't need it to search online. Besides, I don't want to carry it around with me all day at school. What if more shades show up and try to grab it?"

"They seemed more interested in you than the book."

"Yeah, but maybe it was because I had the book."

"I really don't see what an old book would have to do with anything."

"This is why you are less than useless."

"Thanks a lot."

"No problem."

After four excruciating hours of class, during which Walter did not stop talking, it was finally time for Charlie's lunch period. Sixteen foldout tables with connected benches lined the cafeteria floor. Each of the tables held a collection of students. There was the popular table. The sporty one. The nerdy one. And so forth. Charlie sat in his usual spot at the table closest to the entrance. There were other students seated at the same table. Though he didn't exactly consider them close friends, Charlie liked them well enough, and they would share an occasional conversation.

"What's *her* name?" Walter asked as a cute blond-haired girl pranced past Charlie's table.

Charlie groaned. "Melissa Bitner," he mumbled. "And please stop asking me people's names. I can't answer you when everyone's looking." His voice had taken on an almost pleading tone.

Walter had been firing a barrage of questions almost nonstop since entering the school. According to him, Cunningham Middle had a far superior selection of hotties than his own school.

"Melissa Bitner," Walter echoed. "She have a boy-friend?"

Once Melissa was out of earshot, Charlie answered. "Yes, I'm her boyfriend. We've been going steady since I was four."

"Seriously? No. You're lying."

"Man, you're a tough one to trick. I'm sure she has a boy-friend, not that I care." Opening his sack lunch, Charlie took out his food and jabbed his straw into his box of lemonade. He unwrapped a pimiento cheese sandwich on dark rye bread and took a bite.

"Ugh, why are you eating that?" Walter asked as Charlie chomped the sandwich, smacking his lips.

"Because it's delicious," he answered. Two girls sitting on Charlie's side of the bench looked up from their meals. Charlie fumbled with the sandwich. He was going to alienate himself from the other kids even more than he already was, if it kept looking like he was talking to himself. "You can't smell it or taste it anyways. What do you care?" he said very softly, without moving his lips.

"I still have eyes, and that looks disgusting!"

"Psst! Watch out, Charlie," whispered a boy named Terry Romans who was seated diagonally across the table.

Charlie's eyes widened, and he understood the warning just as someone sat down with a thud in the seat next to him. A brute with a flattop and beefy arms slid the rest of Charlie's lunch out of reach.

"Hello, Charlie Doo-doodle," Mo said as he plucked the half-eaten sandwich from Charlie's hand and smashed it into a ball. "Having cheese again for lunch?"

Three other boys sat down too, flanking Charlie from

every angle. All of them wore similar clothing: dirty, grass-stained football jerseys and cargo pants.

"Who are these guys?" Walter asked. "Are they bullies? I hate bullies. I used to get picked on too, up until the moment I decided to pound the next person who shoved me. You've just got to set them straight. That's all. Once they realize messing with you will cost them a black eye or a fat lip, they'll stop bothering you."

Oh, that's all? Charlie wanted to say. All he needed to do was pound Mo, and the bullying would stop? How perfectly simple. Walter was *full* of great ideas.

"Were you trying to make us look stupid yesterday?"

Charlie shook his head. "I wouldn't even know how to do that."

Mo's eyes narrowed. "You're still trying to be funny?"

"Tell them to go walk in front of a truck," Walter ordered.

"Did you hear me, Doo-doodle?" Mo pressed his pointer finger into Charlie's shoulder. "No one thinks you're funny. Everyone thinks you're weird."

The other boys snickered, but Charlie held his tongue. It wasn't worth causing another scene. Why hadn't Mo gotten bored with picking on him already? There were plenty of other kids just as weird as him.

"What's your problem?" a female voice asked from behind their backs. Everyone spun around, including Charlie. Melissa Bitner stood with a couple of other popular girls, scowling at Mo and his band of thugs. "Don't you have anything better to do than bother people?"

"Whoa, dude!" Walter whispered in amazement. "Your girlfriend has come to the rescue."

Charlie gritted his teeth. *Shut up!* he said to himself.

Mo's mouth pulled wide with a grin and he elbowed Wheeler sitting next to him. "I'm not bothering anyone."

"You and your little followers." She glared at Wheeler, who snorted with laughter. "You just walk around looking to mess with people. It gets old."

Mo shrugged. "I'm only trying to help Charlie feel better."

Melissa put her hands on her hips. "Feel better about what?" she asked.

"About wetting himself." Mo snatched Charlie's lemonade off the table.

"You better move!" Walter tried to warn him, but it was too late. Mo squeezed the box and poured lemonade into Charlie's lap.

Charlie tried to get out of the way by scooting back on the bench, but instead he slipped and fell to the floor. Mo stood up and finished emptying the box onto Charlie's pants. It wasn't really cold, but it was wet, and in the most inconvenient location.

Wheeler, Oswald, and Vincent fell off the bench as well, laughing hysterically.

Mo waved his hands to get the attention of everyone else in the cafeteria. "Look! Charlie wet his pants!"

The rest of the students set aside trays and lunch boxes and craned their necks to look over at the commotion. Charlie's face flushed red as he heard their laughter.

Mo shook his head in mock disappointment. "This isn't kindergarten, man," he said as he tossed the box over his shoulder. "You can't just be wetting your pants whenever you want to."

"You're an idiot!" Melissa said. "It's okay, Charlie. No one thinks you wet your pants."

But hearing her defend him in front of everyone else just made everything worse. Scrambling to his feet, Charlie ran out of the cafeteria and headed straight for the bathroom.

Skipping School

"I told you that was going to happen," Walter said as Charlie dried his pants under the hand dryer. "I saw him reaching for the box. It's a classic bully move."

"Well, you didn't do anything about it!"

"I did! You're just slow to react."

Charlie checked his progress in the mirror, but the lemonade wasn't drying fast enough. A dark wet mark remained.

"You know what I don't get?" Walter asked. "Why did a hot girl like Melissa Bitner stick up for you? Maybe she really is your girlfriend."

"No," Charlie answered flatly. "She's just nice like that. She's nice to everybody."

"Wow. She's amazing! We should try to talk to her today. I could help you not sound like a moron."

"Could you please stop talking about Melissa? I have a real problem here." He pointed to his pants.

Walter giggled. "It looks really bad."

"I know! I can't go to my next class looking like this. I'll be laughed out of the school!"

"Then leave," Walter suggested.

"Okay," Charlie said sarcastically. "Good advice."

"No, I'm being serious."

"I can't cut class."

"Sure you can."

"I wouldn't even know how to. I've never done it before." But he was warming up to the idea. There was no way he could go to his next class looking like this. He stared down once more at the lemonade on his pants and vowed never to bring a juice box in his lunch again.

"Just follow my lead," Walter said confidently. "It's not hard."

"Fine. Let's try it."

With the exception of the janitor and a couple of hall monitors facing the opposite direction, the hallway seemed empty when Charlie quietly pushed open the bathroom door and checked around the corner.

"Okay," Walter whispered, although he didn't need to. "You have to act like you're supposed to be out in the hall-way."

"Explain," Charlie said, wiping his nose.

"Don't creep around. Don't act like you're trying to avoid being seen. That never works, and it only draws attention to you. You'll get caught for sure."

Charlie nodded. That made sense. After grabbing his bag from his locker and stopping for a swig from the drinking fountain, per Walter's instruction, Charlie headed for the cafeteria.

"Slow down!" Walter hissed. A teacher stood between him and the cafeteria, posting announcements on a bulletin board. "Be cool!"

Charlie smiled at the teacher as he passed her, but she paid him very little attention, focusing more on the position of her pushpins in the corkboard. Three minutes later, Charlie was racing along the sidewalk by the front parking lot entrance, headed for home.

"I can't believe I just did that!" He pumped a fist in the air. "Did you do that a lot?"

"Yeah, whenever I needed to," Walter answered. "But you can't get careless. Teachers don't notice if you're gone a class period or two every now and then, but they'll pick up quick if you make it a habit."

"Believe me, I won't make it a habit. But I've never felt so alive!" Charlie practically skipped.

"Way to rub it in."

"Oh, sorry."

Several dark clouds gathered overhead, blotting out the afternoon sun. A storm was brewing, and Charlie gave a satisfied sigh. "I love it when it rains, don't you?" Thunder, lightning, the feel of raindrops on his face . . .

Walter moaned, and Charlie understood. "Did you feel anything when the lightning struck you?"

But his Agent never had a chance to answer. As Charlie rounded the corner at a stoplight, his neighborhood just coming into view, the rain began to pour. And Charlie's feet skittered to a stop.

Halfway between him and his apartment, in the middle of the road, stood a red gorilla with horns.

Sanctuary

"What the heck is that?" Walter screamed.

Charlie didn't answer. He was holding his breath and couldn't move a muscle.

The creature wasn't really a gorilla, but it resembled one, with gold slits for eyes, jet-black claws, and a pair of sharp horns curling from its skull. Charlie stood paralyzed as the creature flicked its forked tongue and leapt on top of a parked car. Nostrils flaring and glistening with some sort of glowing, demonic snot, the beast sniffed the air. Then it spoke with a voice that echoed through the core of Charlie's body.

"Leave from it. Break free!"

"I think we should leave now," Walter said.

"Unattach!" the creature commanded, striding forward with arms outstretched.

Before Charlie could run, a clawed hand shot out and

penetrated his chest. From inside Charlie's body, Walter screamed in agony. Charlie could actually feel him writhing.

"It's burning me!" Walter shouted.

Petrified, Charlie looked down, expecting to see a bloody mess, but the creature's claws vanished into his skin. Judging by Walter's continuous screaming, the creature was torturing him. Charlie tried to grab its shoulders, but his hands passed through as though the creature were made of thick red vapor.

"Please!" Walter begged, gasping for air.

"What's it doing?" Charlie asked, but he knew the answer. The claws continued to work into his body, trying to pull Walter out.

"Just run!" Walter yelled. "It burns so bad! You need to run!"

Charlie's heart drummed in his chest. He stumbled backward as the creature took another swipe, fingertips barely grazing his skin. Turning on his heel, Charlie ran in the opposite direction from his apartment.

"Don't stop! Try to lose it!" Walter breathed more steadily now.

"How?" Charlie spat out the word through his panting. He didn't have an athletic bone in his body.

The creature galloped behind, snarling. "Get out! Get out!"

"Is it talking to you or me?" Charlie shouted.

"Me," Walter answered. "Definitely m— There! Just up ahead!"

Less than a hundred yards away, a white steeple jutted

up from a redbrick building with a sign reading HOUSE OF WORSHIP. The creature made a final swipe with its claws as Charlie leapt off the road and scampered up the lawn toward the entrance of the church.

Charlie looked back toward the road and watched as the creature smacked against an invisible barrier and tumbled backward. A few rays of sunlight broke through the rain clouds, and Charlie could see wispy plumes of steam rise from the horned ape's skin as it lay, dazed, on the concrete. It stood slowly, blinking bewilderedly as it searched for the wall. Then it raised one of its claws but hesitated before touching the barrier.

The creature's eyes found Charlie standing on the lawn. Its arms flexed, and its claws balled into fists. "Where will you go?" it snarled. "I can wait forever, you know." But even as it spoke, the creature looked miserably skyward, and, with a puff of red smoke, the monster vanished.

"That was close," Walter whispered.

"*That* was a demon," Charlie said.

"It felt like someone had reached down my throat and was tugging my insides back up."

"Geez!" Charlie stood and walked to one of the church's beautiful stained-glass windows. He had never been inside the building, but he had seen people attending service there on Sundays. The rain began to pour once more, and Charlie ran up the church steps to duck under the eave that jutted out over them.

"How did you know to come here?" he asked Walter. How many books and magazines had Charlie read? Hundreds? There was always a chapter about safe zones. Areas where creatures couldn't enter. Sanctuaries. He should've thought to use the church as a safe zone.

"Just a lucky guess. I saw something about it in a movie." Walter fell silent for a moment. "So, seriously, who did you tick off in the Underworld?"

Charlie flinched and looked once more at the church. "What do you mean by that?"

"Everything from the dark side is trying to get you. I don't think that happens too often."

"That demon attacked *you*," Charlie said defensively, stepping off the front steps of the church and back onto the lawn as the rain let up once more.

"It was trying to get rid of me, not kill me. Didn't you hear it?"

"So? What makes you think this is my fault?" Charlie folded his arms and jumped when a stray cat shot out of one of the bushes. "My life was fine until you showed up."

Walter laughed, and Charlie imagined the sarcastic look on the Guardian Agent's face. "We both know none of what you just said is true. I showed up in time to save your butt."

Charlie stomped toward the sidewalk, but stopped at the edge of the lawn, checking either direction for signs of demons. He knew Walter was right. That demon had been interested in trying to get rid of Walter. And there could be only one reason for that: to attack Charlie. Walter must be protecting him somehow.

Charlie made his way through his neighborhood and to his bedroom without any other incidents. Inside his bedroom, he walked straight to his bed and tentatively lifted his pillow. The peculiar brown book with indecipherable writing was lying just where he'd left it.

"We're lucky it's still here," Charlie muttered. "If the demons wanted it so badly, why didn't they just take it while I was at school?"

"They probably thought you took it with you. I bet that's why that demon was waiting for you in the neighborhood."

"Yeah, maybe."

The box springs groaned in protest as Charlie plopped onto his bed and sifted through a couple pages, thinking things through. He noticed an unsettling silence in his room. Normally, he could hear the methodical hum of his alarm clock, or the air conditioner kicking on and rattling the vents. The Dewdles' apartment complex had been built in the seventies, and the wooden floorboards naturally popped.

No sounds. No disruptions. Just silence.

Charlie stood and walked to the study. He'd missed computer lab, but maybe Walter was right. What his parents didn't know couldn't hurt them. Charlie grasped the door handle and started to turn it, but it stuck.

"I can't believe they locked the door! I thought they trusted me," Charlie moaned.

"Guess they know better."

Charlie rubbed his chin in thought. "I'll ask my Spanish teacher tomorrow if she recognizes the language."

"That's almost twenty-four hours away!"

"Do you have any better ideas?"

Walter did not. At the moment, it would have to do.

Old Maid

Hoonga and Trutti sat at a table playing a rousing game of Bones. Unfamiliar to human beings, the game of Bones was played a lot like Jenga. Players took turns and attempted to remove pieces from a tower. The first player to knock over the tower lost. But unlike Jenga, instead of using a stack of wooden blocks, the game was played with actual bones. Fingers, toes, and ribs worked the best.

In general, demons despised any human recreational activity. Sports, arts and crafts, painting, and games made Underworld creatures squirm with discomfort. Hoonga always kept plenty of games on hand whenever the situation necessitated some good old-fashioned torture. Though he would never admit it, the Cyclops had actually grown quite fond of playing a few of them, but he had to make some minor tweaks to disguise them from the other demons.

Hoonga clamped a hand over his lips to stifle a laugh as

Trutti selected a rib near the bottom of the stack. The tower of bones toppled over on the table.

"No!" Trutti whined. "Not again! I really thought I would win this time!"

"So did I." Hoonga nodded sympathetically as he spun the Punishment Wheel. The dial landed on "Ears," and Hoonga blew a billowing puff of fire. Howls and cackles ensued from Trutti and Hoonga, respectively, as red flames ignited the demon's tiny head.

"One more game!" Hoonga insisted, rubbing his meaty paws together. "Come on, Trutti." He made a pouting face as the tortured demon extinguished the flames from his bat-like gray ears. "Just one more. I promise to let you win this time."

"You said that last time," Trutti huffed, blinking his yellow eyes. "And the time before that and at least a thousand times before that!" He sucked the saliva from his buckteeth back into his mouth.

"I can't help it if you haven't figured out which pieces to pick. There's a strategy. Look, if you'll be a good sport, I'll teach you how to play and win."

Trutti stared at the pile of bone pieces and scrunched his nose.

Just then, a knock sounded from the door at the top of the staircase, and Hoonga's eye narrowed. He nodded at Trutti, who eagerly cleaned up the game pieces and shoved them back into their box.

"Come in, Gorge!" Hoonga bellowed.

The door opened and a red apelike demon with horns

sauntered timidly onto the first step of the staircase. "Master Hoonga, I—" Gorge started to speak, but Hoonga cut him off.

"Come down here!" he snarled. "Don't make me strain my ears."

Gorge hung his head, horns sparking against the stone handrail as he tromped to the bottom.

"Now," Hoonga said once Gorge stood cowering in front of him. "Give me your report."

"I ran into a problem with the boy," Gorge blubbered.

The Cyclops folded his arms and sat on the edge of his desk. Trutti scampered up onto Hoonga's shoulder.

"The boy is aided by some sort of familiar. A guardian spirit. One of the Afterlife Academy Agents, I believe. The shades warned me about it, but I didn't think it would still be there when I arrived." Gorge glanced around the room, and his eyes focused momentarily on several rusted torture racks. Known for his zero-tolerance policy when it came to failures, Hoonga always kept his torture racks oiled and ready for use.

Hoonga followed Gorge's gaze and smiled. "You're not making any sense, Gorge. Please explain."

Gorge looked away from the horrifying devices. "Uh . . . the boy. Some spirit guides him from the inside."

"Yes, yes, I know. You just explained that. What happened next?"

"I tried to pull the spirit out, but it resisted, and then . . ." His head drooped, and Hoonga jabbed a black claw under Gorge's chin so that Gorge was forced to look him in the eye.

"You let him get away?"

"I let him get away." Gorge let out a sob. "He made it to a sanctuary. I didn't anticipate that. I toyed with the boy for a bit. Had a little fun. Thought I would chase him around until he wore out, and then I could have an easier time with him. But I wasn't quick enough. And once he made it to the church, I was powerless, you know. I was this close." Gorge held up his thumb and forefinger to give Hoonga a visual. "I tried, master, but I failed."

Hoonga sighed. "Indeed you did."

"But I will try again," Gorge quickly spoke. "Next time there's a storm. The very next time, I will go, and I will not fail you. You'll see. I'll—"

"Ah, but you see, there's no more rain in the forecast for the next few days." Hoonga clamped his hand on Gorge's shoulder and squeezed. "That's why your attack was so important. I think I was very clear with you when I gave you this assignment."

Gorge groaned. "I know, I know. Give me another chance, boss. Let me make this up to you."

"Oh, absolutely!" Hoonga nodded.

"Really?"

"Of course. But not in the way you're probably hoping. What do you think, Trutti?" He peered up at the smaller demon. "How should we let Gorge make it up to us?"

Trutti was nibbling on a wiry fingernail. He snapped his fingers and began to chant, "Let's play . . . Old Maid, Old Maid, Old Maid!"

Hoonga's eye brightened. "Excellent idea!" He forced Gorge to turn around and face a twisted metal table. Covered in stains, it had razor-sharp edges and had been created with one purpose in mind: absolute torture. A single deck of musty playing cards sat in the center of the table.

Gorge whimpered. "Not Old Maid. Anything but that!"

Hoonga clicked his tongue. "Oh, come now, you know you want to play."

"I do not!" Gorge insisted.

Hoonga ignored the red demon as he took up his deck of playing cards. Trutti continued to chant from atop Hoonga's shoulder, growing louder and louder. Old Maid was by far the worst game and caused the greatest amount of anguish for Hoonga's victims.

After a rousing, or torturous, depending on your perspective, game of Old Maid, Gorge was free to go.

An hour later, the intercom buzzed, and the sniveling voice of Hoonga's secretary filled the room, temporarily breaking Hoonga's concentration.

"Master Hoonga?" the voice inquired.

"Yes, Tharice, what is it?" Hoonga responded.

"I have a message for you."

"Go on."

"Someone will be paying you a visit later this evening to discuss an important matter," Tharice said.

Hoonga's eye twitched. "Who said this?"

The static crackled on the intercom. "I apologize," Tharice said. "He wouldn't give me his name. But he did say you would be expecting him."

The intercom fell silent, but Hoonga didn't move.

"What is it, master?"

"Not now, Trutti." Hoonga walked to his desk. "I need time to think. Leave me for a while."

"Leave you? You want me to *go*?" Trutti asked in disbelief.

Without another word, the enormous Cyclops shooed Trutti off his shoulder, and the lesser demon darted from the room.

20

Dead Language

Charlie weaved his way through the crowded hallway toward his Spanish classroom. He felt awkward and exposed with the weight of the unusual book sagging in his backpack. All around him, kids whispered to one another at their lockers, and he wondered if they were still talking about what had happened yesterday with Mo.

"Look!" Walter cheered. "It's your girlfriend!"

Charlie looked up, then quickly ducked his head. Melissa Bitner, perfect ponytail whipping behind her in slow motion, was walking straight toward Charlie.

"She's looking right at you!" Walter's voice was filled with glee.

"No she's not," Charlie muttered under his breath. "She's probably—"

"Hey, Charlie." Melissa stood in front of him, hugging her chemistry textbook to her chest. "I feel bad about what happened yesterday. Are you okay?"

She was all by herself. Where were the other popular girls who usually followed her around? Charlie had never shared an actual one-on-one conversation with Melissa before.

"Uh . . . um . . . I . . . have Spanish class." They were the only words he could piece together in his mind.

"Oh my gosh," Walter groaned. "You are horrible. Just say something normal to her."

"Mo thinks he's so cool because he can pick on people," Melissa said. "But he's really just a big idiot."

Charlie swallowed.

"Come on! Don't do this. Just agree with her. Nod or something!" Walter pleaded in Charlie's ear.

"Yeah . . . you're right," Charlie managed to say. "He is an idiot." He kept his eyes glued to the floor and Melissa's light-blue flip-flops.

"That wasn't so bad, now, was it?" Walter asked.

Melissa laughed. "So, are you heading to Spanish class? Is that what you said? Who's your teacher?"

Charlie found an ounce of courage and raised his eyes, but only halfway. He ended up staring at Melissa's painted fingernails and her chemistry book. "I have Mrs. Morales."

"Oh, I heard she's tough."

"She's not so bad," Charlie answered, relaxing a bit. "She just sometimes—" He stopped short and stared at Melissa's arm. That was odd. Where did she get that bracelet? Had she always worn it? He'd never noticed it on her before.

"Here we go again." Walter's voice snapped Charlie from his trance. "How many times are you going to make her say your name over and over before you answer?"

"Charlie?"

Charlie finally realized Melissa was speaking, and he dropped his eyes once more to the floor. "I better get to class," he mumbled.

"Yeah, me too." She moved to the side, and Charlie shuffled past.

"What happened?" Walter asked. "Do you always freeze up when you talk to girls? That's a real problem. If you would just listen to me, I could help you not act like such a doof."

"I don't need your help," Charlie said, pausing at the drinking fountain. He took a gulp of water and glanced around. "I froze up because I noticed something about her. Something weird."

"What kind of weird?"

"She was wearing a Spirit Spy bracelet."

"A what?"

"Spirit Spy is Wisdom Willows's trademarked brand. The same geometrical design is stamped on all his merchandise. T-shirts, excavating gloves, jewelry. Melissa's bracelet had that symbol!"

"Whatever, man. It probably just looked a lot like a spirit—whatever you called it—bracelet."

"I think *I* would know what it looks like, okay? I've seen that design hundreds of times on SpiritSpy.org. That was definitely one of Wisdom Willows's products."

"Well, I bet she doesn't even know what it stands for."

"I guess so." Still, where would Melissa find a bracelet like that? It wasn't like they were sold at the mall.

"*¿Sí, Charlie, puedo ayudarte?*" Mrs. Morales asked as Charlie approached her desk. The bell had rung a minute earlier, and all of Charlie's classmates had already left.

"Um, yeah, um . . . what?" Spanish was not Charlie's best subject.

"May I help you?" she translated.

"I was wondering if you know what language this is written in." Charlie unzipped his backpack and removed the book. It thudded loudly against the desk.

Mrs. Morales frowned at the dirty cover and ripped several tissues from the box next to her mug of pens. After wiping most of the dirt clean, she flipped open the cover and raised an eyebrow. "Is this from the library?" she asked.

"Yes . . . I mean, no. Uh . . ." Charlie stumbled over his words. "It's not from the school. I checked it out from Gabbiter Public Library."

"Well, it's definitely not Spanish or any language I've ever seen before," she said.

"Can you read any of it?"

She wiped one of the pages with another tissue and narrowed her eyes. After several more flips, she sighed. "I'm afraid not. I would assume it's written in some sort of dead language."

"Oh, snap!" Walter shouted.

Charlie jerked back in surprise and nearly knocked over the plant on his Spanish teacher's desk. Mrs. Morales gasped, and Charlie quickly faked a sneeze.

"Sorry!" Charlie apologized, wiping his nose. "I think I have a cold."

"It's all right," she said.

"Did you hear her?" Walter still spoke with a blaring voice. "A dead language? We were right!"

Charlie glared down at the floor and shook his head.

"If she knows it's written in a dead-people language, maybe she's a paranormal geek too. Ask her why the demons want it so badly," Walter continued.

"Be quiet," Charlie hissed.

"Excuse me?" Mrs. Morales peered over her glasses.

"Sorry, I didn't mean you. Thanks for your help." Charlie collected the book and walked hastily out of the classroom.

"Why did you tell me to be quiet?" Walter asked once they were out in the hallway. "And why did you leave without asking her about the demons? Go back in there!"

Charlie stomped his foot. "She wouldn't know what I was talking about, and she would probably think I was crazy!"

"She said 'dead language.' Weren't you listening?"

"A dead language is a language no one uses anymore. Like Latin! And demons aren't dead. They're not zombies!"

"Oh," Walter said softly. "I didn't know that."

"Obviously!"

"What are we going to do now?"

"I don't know. Maybe there's another teacher I could talk to. Someone at the high school." Charlie hurried past several students, but he didn't care if they could hear him apparently talking to himself.

"Don't go to another teacher. They won't know," Walter said. "What you need to do is scan the pages onto your computer."

Charlie scoffed. "Oh, okay, you're *so* brilliant."

"You could then upload them onto your dorky website and ask your friend Mr. Willow what he thinks it is."

Charlie started to twirl his finger next to his ear, but stopped short. "That's actually a good idea."

"No kidding. Don't you have computer lab after lunch?"

"Not today. It's only twice a week, and I'm still not allowed on the computer at home."

"So? Just wait until they go to sleep tonight and sneak into the office. Your parents forgot to lock the door this morning after you fed your birds."

Of course Walter had noticed that. But it was another good idea. All of a sudden, Walter was full of them. Or was he? Why wasn't Charlie able to think straight anymore?

Charlie's shoulders drooped. Cutting class. Sneaking out of his room. Going behind his parents' backs. He sighed and shook his head.

"You're turning me into a criminal."

Shadow Speech

Later that night, when everyone else in the apartment had fallen asleep, Charlie tiptoed down the hallway and slid into the study. Immediately, the squadron of birds erupted.

"Shut them up, man!" Walter ordered.

Charlie quickly divvied out heaping handfuls of bird feed into each of the cages. The birds fell quiet, except for an occasional chirp as they ate.

"Why not a hamster or something awesome like a snake?" Walter asked. "Those dumb birds would drive me crazy."

Charlie didn't respond, but went to work scanning several pages of the book onto the computer. Within a few minutes, he'd successfully uploaded them onto SpiritSpy.org. After adding labels and posting a series of questions, Charlie sat back and waited for the answers to come.

The first few comments arrived from unknown sources and provided zero help.

who's the author? one of them asked.

"Duh, it's written in gibberish, moron!" Walter laughed.

that's obviously spanish, said another.

"You're obviously an idiot," Walter fired back.

Charlie swatted a hand at his ear. "Stop making fun of them. They're trying to help."

Suddenly, a private message popped up.

Looks like Shadow Speech to me. Is this
from that book you found? How high are
your EMF readings?

"Look who it's from!" Charlie practically squealed, then reread the message. "Shadow Speech?"

"Heard of it before?" Walter asked.

Charlie typed a response.

What sorts of books contain Shadow
Speech?

The answer came after a few seconds.

Demonic books. Likely you've found an
old tome containing instructions for
warding off demons.

"This guy's weird," Walter muttered. "I don't like how he talks."

"He's typing. And don't call him weird. I've read everything he's ever written. The man's a genius! His reputation is worldwide." Charlie had in fact read almost every article he had written and patterned his own research style after Wisdom's.

Would those types of books draw the interest of demons and dark spirits? **Charlie asked.**

If by "draw interest" you mean
"entice"—no, I don't think so. You're
probably safe. Spirits from the Underworld rarely make a fuss over books.

"Well, that doesn't help us," Walter said.

Charlie held up his finger for silence as the stranger on the computer added another message.

The only instances I know in which demons are enticed by literature are when
people have stumbled across the most
famous Shadow Speech book of all. Which
is, of course, *The Summoner's Handbook.*
So don't worry.

Charlie looked up from the computer and spun around, staring at the book on the desk. *The Summoner's Handbook.*

"Which is . . . ," Walter probed.

"The book all dark creatures want. It basically holds the secrets of how to create doorways they can use to enter our world."

"That's stupid," Walter said. "That demon we saw the other day was already in our world. It didn't need a book."

Charlie shook his head. "Typically, demons are invisible

to human eyes. Most people don't even know they exist. They're strong in their own realms, but when they come here, they can't do much. They're not that powerful."

"Not powerful? That thing was burning me!"

"You have to be made up of something the demon can touch. I didn't feel much even when it put its hands in my chest. But by opening a gateway, demons can enter our world and walk around like they belong here. Imagine what that demon could have done if it had been running at a hundred percent. *The Summoner's Handbook* would make that possible."

"Do you really think that's *The Summoner's Handbook*?"

Charlie reached over to touch it, but stopped before his fingers grazed the cover. "Maybe."

"And it just so happens, the most dangerous book in the world has been buried all this time in a hole behind a shopping mall?"

"I know it sounds ridiculous. But this book contains Shadow Speech. And things have been trying to attack us to get at it."

"How can we know for sure?"

Charlie dropped his hands and typed a message to Wisdom Willows.

How would I know if I've found *The Summoner's Handbook*?

You haven't. Trust me, Wisdom answered.
But how would I know? Charlie jabbed back.
Two minutes passed before a long answer appeared.

You have to be careful. Don't go trying to recite any passages out loud. Shadow Speech books have a decoder page at the back, so I've heard, that contains characters much smaller than the rest of the writing. Stare at these words for three minutes, and you will be able to read them. Then you will understand the book in its entirety. If it is indeed *The Summoner's Handbook,* you'll know by the author's name on the cover. Igor Yad. He wrote only one book. Let me know what happens.

Walter whistled.

Charlie slumped in his chair. "Should I do it?"

"What could it hurt?"

"What if something happens like before? What if that creepy woman spirit—er, the banshee—shows up and tries to grab me again?"

"I'll yell the secret word, and then you'll know to stop reading," Walter said.

"What's the secret word?"

"Idiot! Stop reading!" Walter answered.

Charlie smiled and turned the book to the back page. Goose bumps rose on his arms as he saw much smaller characters. He became completely still as he stared at the pages. After several minutes of focusing, a slight tremor shook his hands. The written characters on the paper began to shift into different positions. Charlie froze and watched as the once-unrecognizable marks stretched and formed words he could clearly read.

A Wraith in the Road

"You all right?" Walter asked, but Charlie made no answer. "Grunt if you can hear me," he ordered.

Charlie grunted.

"Good. Can you read anything yet? Grunt once for no, twice for yes."

Charlie grunted twice.

"Oh boy."

Charlie slowly closed the book and stared down at the cover. His breathing sped up.

"Can you read that, too?" Walter asked.

Charlie grunted twice again.

"Stop grunting. You don't have to grunt anymore. Just answer me!"

"Yes, I can read it."

"And?"

"Igor Yad," Charlie answered.

"No way!"

"Can *you* read it?" Charlie asked.

"No. Nothing happened when I stared at that page."

"Maybe it's because you're dead," Charlie reasoned. He reopened the book and glanced at the pages. Eerie hand-drawn images now appeared as he riffled through. Images that hadn't been there the other times he'd looked at it. Each of the pages contained spells or instructions on how to perform some sort of demonic ritual.

"What's it say? No, wait, don't tell me!" The air in the room grew thick and stagnant. The birds stopped eating, but they made no noise other than the light fluttering of their wings.

"Walter," Charlie whispered. "I'm scared."

"Me too. Let's figure out how to get rid of this."

Charlie returned his fingers to the keyboard.

"You really don't think he waited around, do you?" Walter asked.

Charlie shrugged and typed a short phrase.

You still there?

Yes, Wisdom Willows answered almost immediately. What did you find out?

Charlie typed a one-word response.

Bingo.

You're sure it's *The Summoner's Handbook*? Wisdom asked.

It's written by Igor Yad.

This is huge, Wisdom responded after a second's pause. That is a dangerous book. You can't keep it.

Should I bury it back in the hole where I found it?

No. Don't do that. It's not that simple,

Wisdom typed. Burying the book in the hole won't be sufficient. Someone will just find it again. Maybe we should meet up somewhere. I'd be willing to pay for travel expenses just to take a look for myself. Where do you live?

"Excellent!" Charlie rubbed his hands together. "I can't believe Wisdom Willows is going to help us!" He reached down for the keys, but Walter raised his voice.

"Don't tell him where you live! What if he's some sort of psycho?"

Charlie laughed. "He's not a psycho!"

"Charlie, listen to me. Giving out your address is a big no-no. Remember Stranger Danger from, like, the first grade?"

But Charlie had already typed a brief message stating his home address. He was about to click the mouse to send when his hand suddenly shot out and knocked both the mouse and the keyboard off the desktop. Charlie looked around to see who had done that. His jaw dropped in shock.

"Plenty more where that came from," Walter said, sounding like a cowboy. "Next time you don't listen to me, I'll crack you upside the head with the monitor!"

Charlie closed his mouth and picked up the keyboard. "I'm sorry, you're right. I got excited. What am I supposed to tell him?"

He didn't have to type anything.

Another message blipped on the screen.

Maybe that's a bad idea. Don't tell me your address. I hope I didn't freak you out. Sorry I asked.

"Ask him where the book came from," Walter demanded.

Charlie typed his question, and Wisdom responded immediately.

The original *Summoner's Handbook* was written over a thousand years ago in Romania. It is believed that Igor Yad, a known demonic sorcerer, developed a unique and previously unheard-of relationship with a banshee.

"Wahoo! I told you banshees existed," Walter erupted.

"You were right. So what? It doesn't mean you know more than me."

"I didn't say that."

But Charlie knew what Walter was thinking.

Wisdom's message continued.

With the help of the banshee, Yad compiled every known summoning incantation, including the Gateway spell, within the book's pages. Centuries of unrecorded wars broke out over the book until it finally vanished from existence in the year 1817. Charlie, if you have indeed discovered *The Summoner's Handbook*, you have found one of the most sought-after treasures in existence.

"Eighteen seventeen?" Walter said. "How old is the mall?"

"It wasn't in the mall." Charlie scoffed. "It was buried next to it."

What do I do now? Charlie typed.

Give me some time to research it. I'll check back in with you in the next day or two.

"We've got to think about our next step," Walter said a few minutes later as Charlie crawled under the covers of his bed. "Don't read any more out of the book, and keep it hidden."

"Stop talking like I don't know what I'm doing," Charlie said, annoyed. "I've been involved in paranormal research for most of my life, and I'm not stupid."

From outside the bedroom window, something screamed.

Charlie shot up and kicked the sheets completely off the bed. "Did you hear that?"

Walter groaned. "Yes. Please tell me that was just one of your birds."

Inching toward the window, Charlie peeked through one of the slats of his blinds. A shadowy figure stood below, on the street. Its red robes flickered behind it in the breeze like tendrils of smoke. Dangling on each side were long claws scraping against the asphalt.

"It's a wraith!" Charlie whimpered.

The wraith didn't move much, only hovering in the air a

couple of feet off the ground. But there was no mistaking where it was staring. Charlie took a deep breath and released it slowly through his nostrils. "It's okay. Wraiths are very dangerous out in the open, and they've been known to physically attack humans in certain conditions, but they can't pass through doors or windows. We should be safe in here."

One of the wraith's claws pointed toward the window, beckoning Charlie to come down with a rhythmic flick of its finger.

"It can't come in here," Charlie said again, closing the blinds and backing away slowly.

"Fine. Then I guess we'll just hang out in your apartment for the rest of your life?"

Charlie shook his head. "No, it'll be gone by morning. Wraiths can't tolerate the sunlight."

"You know way too much about these things," Walter muttered.

"Yeah, but it sure is coming in handy, since you don't know anything. What kind of guardian angel *are* you?" Charlie climbed into bed and burrowed down deep under his sheets.

"For the last time, I'm a Guardian *Agent*," Walter corrected him.

Charlie covered his eyes with his forearm and sighed. Everything he had studied was real. His parents had never believed him. They wanted him to stop fooling around with nonsense and grow up. Boy, had they been wrong. In a matter of a few days, the world as Charlie knew it had changed. In a way, he was excited, but it also meant the world was no longer a safe place to live.

Uninvited Guest

The door at the top of Hoonga's staircase opened, and a hooded figure covered in dark-green robes stood in the entryway. Hoonga watched him approach the desk, turning his head from side to side in search of a chair, his eyes lingering on the wriggling, rolled-up carpet. At last, the figure shook his head and sat on a footrest.

"Not very polite," he commented.

Hoonga shrugged. "You caught me at a bad time. Business, you know."

"*Unfinished* business, from what the shades tell me."

Hoonga's upper lip curled as a snarl hung in his throat. "Don't believe everything a shade tells you," he said, controlling his temper. "Shades are imbeciles."

The cloaked figure made a clicking sound with his tongue. "Yours may be, but mine are well trained. And they tell me you've failed, not once but twice now, at your task."

"I wouldn't call it failing. Not exactly." Hoonga shifted in his chair.

"Hoonga, I hired you because I was told you were one of the best at this line of work. But by the looks of things, I see you've only found time to play." The hood tilted toward the box containing the game of Bones.

"What's wrong with a little recreation now and then? It keeps my head clear. Besides, these things take time." Hoonga drummed his clawed fingers across the desk and then shoved the game of Bones into one of the drawers. "What are you so worried about?"

"What kind of pathetic, worthless—"

"Watch your tongue!" Hoonga rose from his chair, muscles rippling in his arms. He leaned across the desk, lunging for the cloak, but the figure reacted more quickly. He rose and extended his hand from the robe, revealing a large, glowing stone clutched in his fingers.

Hoonga roared in pain and shielded his eyes, retreating back to his seat. "All right, you win. Put that away!"

The figure held the stone out for a few seconds before tucking it back inside the cloak. "Next time I'll stick it in your eye! Don't you get it? This is not just some menial assignment. This is *The Summoner's Handbook*! An opportunity like this only comes around once in a thousand lifetimes, and I'm not going to allow you to sit and squander it away. This book can open the Gateway so that your kind can enter the world outright at full strength. No more being invisible. No more slinking in the shadows. No more cowering away from human beings in your weakened forms!" He stomped his foot on the carpet roll. Whatever was trapped inside released an unnerving cry of pain, thrashed about, then rolled sideways until the carpet collided with the refrigerator.

Hoonga reclined in his chair and yawned. "You're not telling me anything new. What I still don't understand is how you'll gain from this book. You're not from here. You're not one of us."

"I have my reasons." The figure took a cautious step away from the rug and returned his focus to the Cyclops. "You just make sure you follow through with the plan. I need *both* the boy and the book for this to work, and we're running out of time. There are already too many eyes watching my every move. You need to strike again tonight!"

Hoonga shook his head. "Can't. It's not going to be raining in that area for at least a week."

The figure hissed. "So you're not even going to try?"

"I thought you knew the rules. Demons need the atmospheric changes brought on by rainstorms to manifest aboveground. Without it, I can only send shades, and what are they going to do? Whisper the kid to death?"

"What about a wraith or a lesser demon? Can't they go to the surface whenever they want?"

"Some can."

"Then why haven't you sent one?" the figure demanded.

"What good would that do? A full-fledged demon had trouble with the boy. You expect a wraith or a lesser demon to be more successful?"

"What about the banshee? You can use the shades to summon one of those, can't you?"

Hoonga shook his head adamantly. "Only in a thunderstorm. Besides, the boy's Agent is far more troublesome than you led us to believe. As long as the two are linked, we can't use a Dark Omen to bring him to the Underworld." Hoonga picked some meat from his teeth and examined it in the light. "To be honest, I don't see why you can't just go and take the book yourself."

The figure's hands dropped to his sides. "Are you out of your mind? For starters, I would be spotted for sure. And secondly, do you have any idea what is required in order for a non–Underworld dweller to open the Gateway? Even with my stone, it is all but impossible without a demon present."

Hoonga raised his eyebrow.

"As it is, we must entrap a human soul within the pages. The Gateway won't open without it. You know that *The Summoner's Handbook* makes a connection with the first living human it contacts. That bond can't be broken or substituted by anyone else. That's why it was so critical that you use the banshee to bring Charlie *and* the book directly to the Underworld."

A low purr emitted from Hoonga's throat. He blinked his eye slowly and rubbed a thumb along one of his tusks. "Then I guess you'll have to wait for the next thunderstorm."

"Just be ready to do your job when the time comes."

With the visitor gone, Trutti returned to the room and scampered onto the desk. "May I ask you a question, master?" the bat-eared creature asked.

Hoonga's eye still lingered on the office door, his upper lip noticeably quivering. "You may."

"Why don't you just kill it?"

Hoonga's eyelid snapped shut and then opened again

with rapid speed. "What?" He stared down at Trutti. "Kill *him*?" He pointed to the door.

"Yes." Trutti gave a curt nod. "I've never heard of any creature above or below that gets away with saying such degrading words to you. Kill it and then . . . let's eat it." Trutti scratched an itch on the end of his nose.

Hoonga released a deep, low growl, which transformed into belly laughter. He smacked the desk with one gigantic hand, an action resulting in Trutti bouncing to the ceiling. "Oh, you make me laugh! I do want to kill him. But for now, I will tolerate his insolence because he's approached me with an intriguing opportunity. Don't you think it would be nice to run around above ground with full strength? Terrorizing everything in our path? Rain or shine?"

"Yes, but"—Trutti's tiny chest inflated with a sad sigh— "I don't like it. With its robes and its demanding voice. Kill it, please."

"I don't know that I *could* kill him. Not while he controls that large shard of Celestial stone."

"Where did it find such an awful trinket?"

"I don't know, but believe me, if he drops that stone for even one minute, I'll make a move." Hoonga placed his hands behind his head. "But I don't think I'd kill him outright."

"No?" Trutti looked shocked. "Why not?"

"Well, I'd want to have a little fun with him first, of course. Wouldn't you?"

"Ah, yes." Trutti rubbed his hands together quickly.

"Now!" Hoonga reached into the desk drawer. "You'll be pleased with the new assignment I'm giving you, Trutti. It will be fun, I assure you."

Trutti's ears perked up slightly. "Fun? What kind of fun?"

"All in due time. But first, I believe we have a bit of a tournament to finish." Hoonga once again pulled out the Bones game box.

Trutti's ears drooped until the tips grazed the desktop.

Tight Squeeze

"I still think you should've said you were sick," Walter grumbled as they arrived at school. "It's too risky."

"Well, it's not any safer at home. And my mom never lets me stay home unless I have a fever," Charlie whispered. He shoved his locker closed and tightened the strap on his abnormally heavy backpack. The one thing the boys had agreed on was that they shouldn't leave *The Summoner's Handbook* lying around unguarded. "Anyway, there's nothing for us to do until we hear back from Wisdom."

Just then, several pretty girls rounded the corner clutching their textbooks tightly in their arms, with Melissa Bitner walking at the center of the group.

Walter whistled, and Charlie turned an alarming shade of pink. Occupying his time fidgeting with a random combination lock on one of the lockers, he hummed quietly to himself until the girls were out of earshot.

"Why did you do that?" Charlie snapped. "Did you whistle at girls when you were alive?"

"Yeah," Walter said.

"You're lying. I know you're lying." Charlie meandered through the hallways, lugging the heavy load on his back.

"Okay, I never whistled to a girl's face. But those girls are cool! Why don't you ever talk to them? Get to know them?"

"Why would I waste my time? I've got more important things to do."

"Like make videos of shopping malls?"

"Or exorcise a demon out of my head."

Walter laughed but stopped short. "Hey, I'm not a demon." He actually sounded offended.

"Close enough."

During lunch, Charlie nibbled on his pimiento cheese sandwich and thought about *The Summoner's Handbook*. He thought about how he had suddenly been able to read the words, and he wondered what sorts of things he could do with it. He thought about how excited Wisdom Willows had become when he learned that Charlie had found the book. The memory made him chew his sandwich with vigor.

"Please tell me you've been paying attention," Walter said, breaking Charlie out of his deep pondering.

"Paying attention . . ." Charlie stopped when he realized he had started to speak out loud. He quickly covered his mouth with his hand and spoke discreetly while chewing. "Paying attention to what?"

"Your buddy at table number three. No! Don't stare at him!" Walter groaned as Charlie turned to look. Mo Horvath made eye contact, and a satisfied grin spread across his face. Oswald, Vincent, and Wheeler were smiling as well.

Charlie swallowed the gooey mass of pimiento cheese. "Great."

"Yep. Recognize that look?" Walter asked. "That's the look someone gives when they plan on pounding somebody. I've given that look many times."

"Mo always has that dumb expression on his face." Charlie stuffed his uneaten Doritos and carrot slices into his crumpled paper bag and dropped it on top of *The Summoner's Handbook* in his backpack.

"You're as good as dead, my friend," Walter said.

"Shut up, shut up, shut up!" Charlie hissed.

"I could help you. I actually have a plan."

Charlie stared longingly at the cafeteria exit, but knew he wouldn't have a chance to escape before Mo caught up with him. And running would make him look even more ridiculous in front of the school. "Fine. I'm listening. What do I do?"

"For starters, don't give them access to your juice box," Walter instructed.

"Brilliant."

"Do you really want my advice?"

Charlie nodded.

"Okay. Do and say exactly as I tell you. No exceptions. Can you do that?"

Charlie hesitated with his answer. "I'll try."

"Right, because here they come."

Charlie started to turn around.

"Don't do anything yet," Walter said. "Just . . . just act like you're bored, and don't be afraid to throw out a few insults. I'll tell you what to do when the time comes."

Mo draped his arm over Charlie's shoulder, and his awful breath wafted across his face. The other three goons sat down around them. Mo sat practically on top of Charlie.

"I need some money," Mo said as his hand dug painfully into the pressure point on Charlie's shoulder. "You got any money?"

Wheeler's sniveling voice chattered next to Charlie's right ear. "Get 'im, Mo," he said. "Get 'im!"

Charlie could never figure out why Wheeler had been allowed to go this far through life without receiving similar treatment. If Charlie could be classified as a dork because of his looks, so should Wheeler. He had a heavily freckled face, or maybe they were zits. Whatever they were, Wheeler had a lot of them. Plus, he was practically cross-eyed. But he was mean.

"You don't have any money, do you?" Mo whispered. Charlie slowly shook his head, crumpling from the pain on his shoulder. "You live in those dumpy apartments over on the boulevard, don't you? The ones by the pound?"

"Pound?" Charlie raised an eyebrow. "Oh, you mean the veterinarian clinic. A pound is something completely different."

"Is that right?"

Charlie nodded. When was Walter going to share his brilliant plan?

The other boys sneered, and Wheeler piped up once more. "Hit 'im, Mo. Hit—"

"Shut up, Wheeler," Mo ordered, then turned back to Charlie. "How is it your dad can transport all that money every day, and yet you and your dumb family never get any of it?"

Charlie closed his eyes. He was having a very difficult time acting bored. Insulting his family was going too far.

Charlie cleared his throat. "My dad drives an armored truck for Carmichael. He just delivers the money to banks and stuff."

"Did I tell you to talk?" Mo ground his teeth together.

"You asked me a question." Charlie tried to sound tough.

The goons' lips poked out in shock, and they mouthed the words "Oh no," followed by hysterical laughter.

Charlie wished he had held his tongue. Why hadn't Walter spoken up yet?

"I've got an idea. Why don't we take a walk after school to your place? You could show me where your dad parks his armored truck." Mo peered over Charlie's head, hamming it up for the amusement of his buddies.

"He doesn't park the truck at the apartments. He has to get it from the garage at work." Charlie stared at a smidgeon of cheese stuck to the cafeteria table. Was that cheese from his sandwich, or was it there from a previous lunch? Charlie began to wonder how often the janitor cleaned the tables.

Mo released his pinching grip on Charlie and leaned back in his chair. "You think you're pretty smart, don't you?"

Charlie shook his head quickly. "No. I'm not smart. Oh, wait. Were you comparing me to you?"

Mo's lips curled upward, but his smile wavered. "I guess there's no point talking to you about your worthless dad and his pathetic job. So why don't we just take a walk to the bathroom instead?"

"You ready to do as I say?" Walter piped up. "Okay. Slowly turn, and stare Mo right in the eyes. Don't blink!" he instructed.

Charlie flinched. There was no way he could do that without blinking.

"I'm serious, Charlie. Do it!"

Charlie gulped and followed the command. Mo, laughing at some inside joke Oswald had shared, had his eyes closed. Charlie found himself staring at the pimple-pocked cheek of the overgrown orangutan.

"Whoa, Mo, check him out!" Vincent said. "You made him mad. Look out!" He drumrolled his hands against the table as the suspense began to build.

Mo's eyes leveled with Charlie's.

"Now, repeat after me," Walter said. "Do you think you actually scare me?"

Charlie's jaw felt like it was wired shut, but he pried it open. "Do you think you actually scare me?"

Mo looked baffled. "Yeah, I do." He grabbed Charlie's shirt collar with his free hand and yanked him forward. "In fact, I know I do."

"Grab his hand," Walter said. "Don't hesitate!"

Walter was going to get him killed. But he had gone too far to turn back now. Charlie limply took hold of Mo's hand, and Mo cackled.

"Look, he's trying to hold my hand!"

"Squeeze it, Charlie. Don't hold back," Walter instructed confidently.

Charlie took a deep breath and squeezed.

Crunch.

The sound carried across two cafeteria tables. Several of Charlie's classmates turned to look because of Mo's shriek of pain. He clamped his mouth shut, and his eyes darted back and forth from his hand to Charlie's own shocked face.

"Let . . . go!" Mo gasped.

Charlie wanted to. But Walter wouldn't let him. Just like the night before, Walter was channeling his own energy through Charlie's body. Only now their strength had combined to form a death grip on Mo's hand.

Mo's face turned from white to green to purple. He pulled back his fist that had been gripping Charlie's shoulder for a punch, but appeared to lose momentum. Wheeler slung his arm around Charlie's neck in a tight headlock, trying to wrench him away from Mo.

"Tell them to back off!" Walter ordered.

Charlie immediately obeyed. "Tell your friends to back off, or I'll squeeze harder!" The pain in Mo's eyes scared Charlie, but filled him with confidence.

"Back . . . off," Mo whined. "Back off!"

Wheeler scooted back, letting go of Charlie's neck, unsure of what to do with his hands.

The table crowded with people watching, whispering, and pointing.

"Okay, Charlie. Just so you know, there's a teacher coming over here," Walter warned. "I think it's time to let go."

Charlie could see the cafeteria aide parting the wave

of students. Just before she arrived at the table, Charlie squeezed Mo's hand extra hard. "Next time you touch me, I'll snap your hand off!" Both he and Walter released their grip. "And yours, too!" Charlie turned and pointed at Wheeler's confused face.

Mo stood, clutching his hand close to his chest, his eyes a mixture of pain and rage. Charlie noticed tears in his eyes. Part of him actually wanted to apologize.

"What's going on here?" the aide asked as she walked up.

Charlie couldn't speak. The realization of what he had done was hitting him. His heart raced, his stomach gurgled. If he didn't escape the cafeteria immediately, he was going to have an accident.

"Someone needs to start talking right now!" the aide ordered.

Mo was silent.

"Charlie broke Mo's hand."

"Shut up, Wheeler!" Mo hissed through his clenched teeth.

Wheeler looked puzzled. "But he did, didn't he? Isn't that what—"

"I said, shut up!" Mo's red-rimmed eyes glared at Wheeler, and the sniveling lackey promptly clamped his lips together.

The aide looked from Charlie to Mo. Finally, she sighed. "Okay. Let's get you to the school nurse, and then the office. That looks pretty bad, Mo." Then she spun around and faced Charlie. "You too, Mr. Dewdle. I'm afraid you're going to have to explain yourself to the principal."

"The principal?" Charlie whimpered. "But—"

"No buts. Stand up and let's go."

"Get up, Charlie," Walter said. "Grab your things, but do it like you don't even care."

Charlie stood, fumbled with his backpack strap, tripped over the bench, and had to be supported by Terry and a couple of the other kids still standing close to the table. His knees felt wobbly.

Walter groaned. "That's not exactly what I had in mind."

Charlie muffled a burp and choked back the bile from his stomach. *Don't throw up! Please, don't throw up!* he begged himself. The only time he had ever visited the principal's office was to receive an award for outstanding grades.

"Just get out of the cafeteria before you pass out. And don't look at anybody and . . . uh . . . frown. Like you're mad at the world."

Too many instructions. Charlie needed a pen and paper to take down notes. He did his best to follow Walter's advice, but he suspected he looked more like a lunatic than a rebel.

25

Instant Popularity

"Let me get this straight," Principal Epperson said to Charlie, after he'd talked alone with both Ms. Buttars and Mo. The lunchroom aide sat against the wall watching Charlie like a hawk, her hands folded in her lap.

"Despite what Ms. Buttars has been saying, Maurice has informed me that what happened in the cafeteria was just an accident. He said you had nothing to do with his injury. Do you agree with that?"

Charlie's eyes widened. "Mo said that?"

"Is that not what happened?" Mr. Epperson asked. "Because Ms. Buttars here"—he pointed to the lunchroom aide—"says that she saw you squeezing Maurice's hand."

"I told you already," Mo grunted. "My hand got stuck between the tables. Charlie was helping me get it out."

Charlie shook his head in confusion and tried to process what Mo was saying. "What?" he said, shooting a quick glance over at Mo. Mo's left eye twitched, and Charlie understood the warning.

"Okay, genius. Didn't I say you were in the clear?" Walter's voice sounded in Charlie's mind. "Now agree with Mo, and let's get out of here."

"Uh—um—yeah, that's right," Charlie stammered. "I was just trying to help."

"You're certain? Both of you?"

Charlie and Mo nodded in agreement.

"Mr. Epperson, I was there, and I assure you—" Ms. Buttars argued, but the principal held up his hand.

"I appreciate your bringing this to my attention, but if Maurice says it was an accident, then we should be praising Charlie, not punishing him."

A bug the size of a grapefruit could've flown into Charlie's open mouth and he wouldn't have noticed. How was this happening? He'd thought for sure his days at Cunningham were over.

Mr. Epperson glanced up at the clock above his bookshelf. "Well then, last period will be ending shortly. Maurice, you'll wait here until your mother arrives to take you home. Charlie, you're free to go back to class."

"That was amazing!" Charlie shouted, slamming his locker shut with a vigorous bang.

"Settle down, man. It's not like you did anything that great," Walter said, edginess in his voice. "You know why Mo did that, right?"

Charlie paused. "I think so."

"A whole bunch of your classmates saw what you did to him. He's not going to rat you out to the principal and be known as a tattletale. But eventually, he's going to come after you."

Charlie sighed. Leave it to Walter to ruin the mood. "He'll probably pound me into a bloody pulp. But not if you help me."

"I'm not so sure."

"How did you do that anyways? You were really brilliant!"

"I wasn't planning on doing anything like that, but when he grabbed you, it made me mad. I think when I get mad, I can do things I normally can't. Maybe it channels my energy or something."

"You're like the Hulk! I still can't believe it . . . Mo Horvath! The guy's a monster!"

Walter laughed. "Hey, I probably won't say this too much, but you did pretty good yourself."

Charlie smiled, his eyes unfocused as his memories replayed in his mind, but then he shook the thoughts away. "Whatever. I almost peed my pants." The last bell rang overhead, and Charlie got to his feet.

"I've been thinking about what you and Mo were talking about earlier," Walter said. "I wonder if your dad is involved after all."

Charlie shrugged. "I don't see how this has anything to do with him. He's been a driver since I was a baby."

"Interesting."

"What's so interesting about it?"

The hallways began to fill up with students, and something unusual happened. People actually noticed Charlie and started talking to him.

"Nice job, dude," Terry Romans said as he passed Charlie's locker. "You really gave it to him."

"Thanks." Charlie blushed.

"I heard you broke three of his fingers," said Patrick Dorrell. "And like six of his carpal bones." Patrick had been Charlie's friend in second grade, but they had rarely spoken since.

"You actually *broke* his hand?" a girl's voice asked from behind. Charlie turned and almost dropped his backpack when he saw Melissa Bitner standing by his locker.

"Well, I—not exactly," Charlie stammered. His chest swelled with pride. But only for a moment.

"I thought you were better than that, Charlie Dewdle," she said. Then she flipped a lock of hair behind her ear, nudged Patrick with her elbow, and pushed off down the hallway.

Charlie didn't know what to focus on—the fact that Melissa Bitner thought what he did was wrong, or the fact that—

"Melissa Bitner knows my name! First and last!"

Walter sighed. "That was definitely the takeaway."

26

Pulling Strings

Alton Tremonton marched along the path leading to Darwin's office. He carried a handful of manila folders, which he straightened whenever his quickened pace jostled one loose. All around him, Afterlife Academy cadets hustled through the arena, firing weapons and running drills, but Alton didn't acknowledge any of them.

"Hey, look! It's that guy from Categorizing! The one with the pig clock," Alton heard one of the younger cadets announce. He pressed forward before anyone else could recognize him.

One day, he told himself. *One day, you'll prove to everyone where you belong. Just be patient.*

"Ah, good. Thank you for coming so quickly," Darwin said as Alton entered the office and walked past the large stone lion.

"Did I have a choice?" Alton sneered.

Darwin managed a slight smile. "Did you bring me what I asked for?"

Alton handed over the stack of envelopes.

Darwin removed a pair of bifocals from his suit coat pocket. "These are the personal files of the most recently Categorized?"

Alton nodded. He glanced around the room and admired the mahogany-colored bookshelves. So many fancy books. Darwin also had a beautiful window that looked out on the massive Academy arena. Alton had none.

Darwin flipped through one of the folders, the shuffling of papers the only sound in the office. "I just don't understand it. This file doesn't indicate anything unusual with this cadet."

"Why would it?" Alton asked dryly.

Darwin glanced up over his bifocals. "Alton, how long have you been administering placement exams? Thirty years, is it?"

Alton shrugged. "Give or take."

"And do you personally vouch for every cadet you send me?"

"What is this about?" Alton leaned forward, trying to see over the edge of the folder in Darwin's hand.

Darwin sighed. "We've run into a little bit of a problem with one of our newer Agents."

"Which one? Do I know him?"

Darwin narrowed his eyes and stared at Alton. "Oh, I think you do. Unfortunately, it's confidential. I'm not at liberty to disclose information on the matter to any unauthorized personnel."

"Well, I *have* applied to the Academy many times. For some reason, the board continually rejects my requests."

"And I bet that's made you angry. Has it not?"

Alton cocked his head to one side. "What are you implying?"

The two held each other's gaze for several intense moments.

Darwin's eyes softened, and he removed his glasses. "Nothing. Nothing. I'm just worried, that's all. I put the lives of others in jeopardy every day with my position. I need to have thorough information about my Agents. I need to feel confident they'll perform to the best of their abilities. You do guarantee my confidence, do you not?"

"That's why I come to work every day," Alton said, but his sarcasm was lost on his colleague. Darwin appeared satisfied by his response.

"Very good. You may go."

Alton swiveled and headed for the door.

"Oh, Alton," Darwin said. Alton stopped and turned. "I saw that you applied once again for Team Leader. It's a coveted position, and there are a number of fine candidates vying for the spot. I'm sure you'd make an excellent choice. I'll pull some strings with the board to see if we can squeeze you in. How does that sound?"

"Sounds like another rejection to me," Alton said as he shoved through the door and exited the office.

27

Tyrone Underhill

That night, the Dewdle family sat down to dinner as usual. Charlie smiled almost nonstop as he slurped each bite of delicious, gooey lasagna. He couldn't get over what he had accomplished that day at school. Charlie had beaten Mo Horvath! And suddenly, everyone had started acting differently around him. He wouldn't go so far as to say he was popular, but besting Mo in the packed cafeteria definitely boosted his chances of no longer being labeled a total geek. Even Melissa Bitner was taking notice. Yes, she seemed annoyed with his methods, but she didn't know what it was like to be in Charlie's shoes every day at Cunningham Middle School. Being picked on. Being ignored. Maybe Walter was right. All Charlie had to do was stick up for himself and his problems with Mo and every other moron would come to an end.

"That's it!" Walter exclaimed in Charlie's ear.

Charlie yelped.

"What's wrong? Is it too hot? Did you bite your tongue?" Charlie's mother asked.

"I'm okay," he mumbled. He had bitten his tongue, but not because of his lasagna's temperature. There had to be other Guardian Agents who handled themselves more appropriately, particularly during a family dinner.

"All right. Just listen to me." Walter's voice returned to normal volume. "I know you can't answer, but I want you to do something extremely important."

Charlie didn't respond. He kept his mouth clamped tight and stared at his dinner plate.

"Sniff once if you understand."

Charlie sniffed.

"Your dad works at Carmichael Armored Vehicles." Walter paused to laugh almost wildly. "This is so awesome! Okay, ask your dad who he works for."

Charlie fidgeted with his fork and scattered a few peas across his plate. He looked at his dad and shook his head. They had a healthy father-and-son relationship, but his dad had come straight from his stressful job—he hadn't even changed out of his uniform—and he enjoyed eating his dinner in peace.

"Just do it!" Walter ordered. "Ask him about his boss!"

Charlie lowered his fork. "Hey, Dad. Who . . . uh . . . who do you work for?"

Mr. Dewdle looked up from his plate, his mouth semi-full of lasagna and salad. "Carmichael Armored Vehicles." Then he took a long gulp of water from his glass.

Charlie nodded and exhaled. "I know that. I meant what's your boss's name?"

"Why?" his dad asked. "Is this some sort of school project or something?"

"Uh . . ."

"Yes! Say yes!" Walter blurted out. "That's a perfect reason!"

"Yeah, we have a homework assignment."

Mr. Dewdle wiped his mouth with a napkin and gestured to his wife to pass the platter of lasagna. "I work for a guy named Howser. Lawrence Howser. He means well, I guess. He's a young guy. Inexperienced. But he has his graduate degree. So . . ."

"That's why you're going to get your master's, dear," Charlie's mom whispered. "So you don't have to put up with what your father goes through every day."

"Right." His dad ladled another heaping serving onto his plate.

"Great! Thanks," Charlie said.

"No, that's not good enough," Walter said. "You need to dig deeper. This could be the breakthrough we need to help us get out of this mess. Ask him who's in charge of Howser. Who's the top guy?"

Charlie scratched his ear, and his knee began to knock up and down against the bottom of the table. "So . . . there's Howser, but who's *his* boss? Who runs the whole company?"

"Of Carmichael? Like the CEO?" Mr. Dewdle asked, before shoveling a forkful into his mouth.

"Yes!" Walter exclaimed.

"Yes!" Charlie exclaimed as well before clearing his

throat and answering in a calmer manner. "The CEO. Exactly. What's that guy's name?"

"The CEO of Carmichael is a man named Sheldon Underhill. He's been there for several years."

"Jackpot!" Walter cheered. "Ask him where he lives."

Charlie whimpered. Really? Did he really have to continue?

"Ask him!" Walter said, unrelenting.

"Where does Mr. Underhill live?"

Mr. Dewdle folded his arms and stared at Charlie; his eyes narrowed with suspicion. "What kind of homework assignment is this? Some kind of career-day project?"

"Sure. I mean, yes," Charlie answered. "We're supposed to learn about corporate businesses and about where their CEOs live."

"Nice one," Walter said.

"Thank you," Charlie replied, failing to catch himself before responding to Walter.

"That's so polite, Charlie. You're learning your manners. You should always say thank you." Charlie's mom beamed as she poured dressing on her salad.

"He owns a big house in Pressley. We went there once for a company dinner. Remember that, Dana?" Mr. Dewdle asked. "They had that indoor basketball court and the swimming pool with that hot-tub grotto."

Mrs. Dewdle's eyes lit up and she smiled. "Oh yes, I remember."

"Okay, Charlie. Last question. Ask him if Mr. Underhill has any kids your age."

Charlie fell silent and shook his head. Enough was enough. Now Walter was just trying to make things uncomfortable for him. What did the age of the CEO's kids have to do with their problem? What did any of this have to do with anything?

"Do it, please!" Walter begged.

"I'm not gonna ask that," Charlie mumbled under his breath, and then covered it up with a loud cough.

Walter released a grunt of frustration. "If you don't, I'll make you throw your lasagna in your father's lap."

Charlie tried to imagine how his parents would react if Walter carried through with his promise.

"Don't test me," Walter warned.

"So, Dad, does Mr. Underhill have any kids my age?" Charlie nudged his fork away from his plate.

"He's got a few kids," Mr. Dewdle said. "Maybe his son is your age. I don't know for sure. . . ." He once again glanced at his wife.

"No, I think Tyrone's in high school, isn't he?" Mrs. Dewdle said.

"Tyrone!" Walter shouted. "That's it! Excuse yourself from the table, and go get on the computer. If your parents catch you, say you're researching for the project."

Charlie breathed a sigh of relief and excused himself.

"Okay, what the heck was that all about?" Charlie sat at the desk, his fingers gently nudging the mouse. The screen saver of random Dewdle family photos disappeared, and Charlie clicked on his folder where he'd saved the pictures from *The Summoner's Handbook*. "We still don't know what to do about this," he whispered, waving the cursor over the pictures. "Demons are going to keep attacking until we figure out what to do with the book. And I don't have any emails from Wisdom Willows. Even *he* can't figure out what to do. How are *we* supposed to?"

"Well, I might just be able to help with that. Do you have a Facebook account?" Walter asked.

"Facebook? Yeah, I guess, but I don't get on there much. And I don't really have a lot of friends."

"Just log on to your account. Trust me."

Charlie did as told, and an awkward picture of him wearing wax vampire lips and dark, drawn circles around his eyes stared down at them. Also staring at them were the words "17 Friends."

"I'd probably have more friends if I—"

"Don't worry about it," Walter interrupted. "I don't care how many friends you have. Search for Tyrone Underhill."

"The CEO's kid? Why do you want to do that?"

"Please, just do it!"

Several different Tyrone Underhills registered in the search field, forcing Charlie to research a few of them before finding a match. Tyrone was a dark-skinned boy of about sixteen. Most of his information had been blocked from public view, but Charlie could see that Tyrone went to Afton High School in the neighboring town of Pressley, Iowa.

"Wow! He's pretty popular," Charlie said, taking note of Tyrone's three thousand friends. "Are you happy now?"

"Is there an address?" Walter asked.

"It doesn't say. That information's blocked."

"I guess that's okay," Walter said. "We'll just have to go find him at the school—hold on, maybe his father's listed in an online directory."

"Okay, I'll check."

"There it is! Sheldon Underhill, Twenty-Two Richfield Lane. We can wait for him to get home after school. Just skip last period and take a transit bus or something. We can look up how to get there from the nearest bus stop."

Charlie leaned back in the swivel chair and stuck his index finger in the canaries' cage. They immediately fluttered down to peck lovingly at his fingernail. "Okay. Now what's so important about this Tyrone guy?"

"Tyrone Underhill is currently being guarded by an Afterlife Academy Agent named Ronald Logan. I know him! I met him right before I came to your place. When I saw your dad's name badge tonight, I finally remembered."

"So what's this have to do with our problem?" Charlie asked.

"Ronald's a fully trained Agent. He knows what to do when demons attack. And maybe he'll have an idea what we should do with *The Summoner's Handbook*. Maybe they teach how to destroy it in the Afterlife Academy."

Charlie leaned forward in the chair. "How good is he?" A hint of excitement rose in his voice.

"He's awesome!" Walter answered. "I guess. I really don't have a clue, but he's had four years of Afterlife Academy training. He has to be better than me."

"That's not saying much." Charlie folded his arms.

"And since I'm so happy about this news," Walter said, "I'm going to ignore that and not make you do something painful to yourself."

Charlie once again navigated to SpiritSpy.org. There was

still no message from Wisdom. He leaned over and unzipped his backpack.

"What are you doing?" Walter asked.

Charlie pulled out *The Summoner's Handbook* and flipped it open on his lap. "Maybe there's something in here that could tell us who keeps attacking us."

"Like the mastermind behind it?"

"Exactly." Charlie began turning the pages and reading the headings. *Befriending Banshees, Enslaving Lesser Demons, Warding Off Angelic Pests.* He smiled. "That could come in handy."

"Don't do anything stupid," Walter warned. "I'm the only one keeping you alive."

"I'm not going to *do* anything. It's just good to know I have options."

The computer chirped as an instant message from Wisdom Willows appeared on the screen.

Charlie held his breath.

How are things going? Wisdom asked.

Charlie flexed his fingers and typed his reply.

Okay, I guess. It hasn't exactly been quiet around here.

What do you mean?

Charlie briefly filled in Wisdom on the demon attack and the appearance of the wraith outside the apartment. He was about to include the part about being possessed by his Guardian Agent, but Walter erupted.

"Don't tell him about me!" Walter shouted.

"Why not? He's just trying to help."

"He doesn't have to know everything. And what if he tries to do some weird voodoo magic to pull me out of you and I end up inside something else? Like one of your dumb birds?"

"He won't do that." Charlie's finger hovered over the mouse.

"I don't want anyone to know about me just yet, and I should have a say in that, don't you think?"

Charlie sighed. "Fine." He deleted the line about Walter and added another question.

```
Have you found out what I should do
about the book?

Not yet. There's not a lot of information
available.
```

"Ask him about how we can find out who's behind the demon attacks," Walter said.

Charlie nodded as he typed, then waited for Wisdom's response.

```
It's difficult to say. The Summoner's
Handbook will draw the attention of
all Underworld creatures, particularly
higher-level demons. You have to under-
stand how dangerous that book is. It's
the holy grail of demonic artifacts.
```

Every dark thing has dreamed about getting their claws on it. I'm impressed you've managed to fend them off so far by yourself, but you won't continue to be so lucky. They'll just become more and more aggressive. My advice would be to stay in your home at all times. I'm close to discovering a way to destroy the book. Until then, don't travel anywhere out of your neighborhood, especially at night.

"That's good advice." Charlie closed the Internet browser.

"Agreed. But we have to make that trip to Pressley."

"You read what Wisdom said. The demons are just going to become more desperate."

"All the more reason to get help from another Agent. Trust me, Charlie, we have to do this."

Trutti's Task

The three shades floated in midair beneath a faded Slumber Inn billboard sign poking above the freeway. Their long black cloaks fluttered and flapped as if caught in a strong wind, though the air in Gabbiter, Iowa, was still. From their position, they could see the front parking lot and pickup zone of Cunningham Middle School.

Down below, lounging on a rock, sat Trutti, picking at his toenails with his teeth. Hairless, with flaky gray skin and a foxlike snout, which he constantly licked with his forked tongue, Trutti was definitely not easy on the eyes. Had he not been invisible to most humans, he would've looked to them like the world's ugliest dog. Everything on his body, except his ears, drooped and sagged. He could stand upright if he chose to, but he preferred walking on all fours. He called to the shades in a bored yet agitated voice.

"Has he left yet?"

"No one has exited the school," one shade replied.

"All is quiet," hissed another. "No, wait! See now. The boy is the first to leave. It hurries out. It trips, but stands again. Just as you said, it leaves well before any others, and it seems to be headed—"

Trutti growled, cutting the shade off midsentence. "Could you cool it with the play-by-play? Does he have the book with him? Is it in his possession?"

The shades paused, peering down upon Trutti and then back toward the school. "We cannot know for sure. But the boy has a pack. Something on its back."

Trutti scampered up the billboard post until he stood just beneath the shades. Looking out over the trees, he narrowed his eyes and watched as Charlie walked quickly away from the school.

"He has it in his possession," Trutti said. "Can't you see its aura?" He pointed at the rippling waves of energy pulsing from Charlie's backpack. "And he's definitely not headed for his home."

"How do you know?" the shades asked.

"Because his home is in the opposite direction!"

The shades turned, silently processing this information. Satisfied, they nodded. "Yes, you are wise."

Trutti rolled his eyes. "Okay. Follow him. Stay close, but don't get spotted."

"Why should we worry about being spotted? It cannot harm us."

Trutti puffed out his cheeks. Next to the tall shades, the lesser demon truly looked like a small, pathetic animal. But with surprising speed and leaping ability, he snagged the cloak of the closest shade, dragging it down through the air until its face floated at eye level.

"Hoonga put *me* in charge here! Do you understand?" Trutti hissed.

The shade nodded its hood and began stammering an apology as the other two lowered next to it. But before it could finish its groveling, Trutti muttered and stuck his hand into the hood, and the shade blinked out of existence with a black puff of dust.

"Master!" the two remaining shades wailed, bowing reverently. "Shade One Hundred Fifteen deserved it! Always it questioned. Always defiant. But not us, Master Trutti. We obey—always obey!"

Trutti rolled his eyes again. "Whatever. Now go and find out what the boy is up to. Don't be seen, and meet me at the rendezvous point tonight once the sun has fully set."

"Yes," the shades acquiesced. Dropping down from the billboard, they kept hidden beneath the cover of trees as they took off after Charlie.

29

Reunion of Sorts

The day after Charlie's victory over Mo was relatively un-eventful. Before he knew it, school was over and he was walking briskly through a part of town he'd never been to before. Most of the buildings were dilapidated. He passed Tebo's Pawnshop and an Asian market. A man walking a rottweiler on a leash approached along the sidewalk. The dog had its hind leg at half-mast over a fire hydrant when it caught wind of Charlie and began to snarl. Charlie instinctively stepped sideways into a parking lot to give the dog and its owner a wide berth.

"All right, let's review the game plan. You have the bus schedule printout?" Walter asked.

"Where else would it be?" But Charlie patted his back pocket just to make sure.

"Okay, okay. I'm just checking. You're acting nervous."

"I'm not nervous!" Charlie snapped. But he was.

Extremely nervous. He and Walter had reviewed the plan several times the night before, but he highly doubted it would work.

When the bus arrived at the bus stop, Charlie boarded the near-empty vehicle headed to the town of Pressley, just a couple of miles away.

The bus stopped in the center of town, and Charlie got out. The neighborhood was quite different from the one he'd just left, and from his own. Beautiful mansions towered over him as he walked the five blocks to the Underhills' residence and waited. Ten minutes later, a jet-black Jeep Cherokee pulled into the driveway.

Tyrone and another high school boy stepped out of the car and onto the lawn. They both wore baseball caps, and Tyrone was talking on a cell phone. A third boy, closer to Charlie and Walter's age and dressed in an odd all-white uniform, emerged from the back of the vehicle. Only he didn't use the door. He simply materialized on the outside of the Jeep as though by magic.

Walter gasped. "That's him! That's Ronald Logan. You've got to move now!"

Charlie sprang from the bench, bolting toward Tyrone.

"Don't run!" Walter groaned. "You're gonna get—"

"Where you going, kid?" Tyrone asked as he noticed Charlie, clicking his phone closed.

Charlie turned and stared at the sidewalk in embarrassment. "Uh . . . me?"

"Yeah, you," Tyrone said. "You don't live around here, do you?"

Charlie forced a laugh and ran his fingers through his hair. "Oh no, I'm just visiting my friend."

"You have to get closer to him," Walter said. "Or I might not be able to get Ronald's attention."

Suddenly, an explosion of purple light enveloped Tyrone. Charlie covered his eyes with his hands as the light shone brighter than anything he had ever seen. He could barely make out Tyrone from behind the purple barrier. It was like looking through murky glass.

"What's wrong with you?" Tyrone asked from behind the bubble of glowing purple light. "You sick or something?"

"What *is* that?" Charlie pointed. "Why is it so bright?"

Tyrone looked genuinely concerned. "Maybe there's something wrong with him," he said to his friend. Ronald moved in front of Tyrone and held his palms together, wearing a determined glare.

"He's making some sort of shield to protect his target," Walter said. "Maybe that means he can see me. Ronald! Hey, Ronald! It's me. Look over here!"

Ronald didn't respond. Instead, he muttered something unintelligible under his breath, and more light erupted from his fingertips, shooting directly at Charlie.

"Get down!" Walter shouted. Charlie felt his whole body lurch forward as the light hurtled overhead. Then he heard screaming and hissing behind him. Two black-robed figures swathed in the purple light were writhing in the air.

Still shielding his eyes, Charlie scrambled to his knees and watched as the shades burst into clouds of wispy black smoke. The shield faded, and Charlie timidly got to his feet.

Tyrone and his friend backed away slowly, looking at Charlie as if he were a rabid squirrel, and entered the house. But Ronald still stood on the sidewalk, brooding with concentration as his eyes scanned the street.

"Where did they come from?" Charlie whimpered.

"I don't know, but hurry! Try and get Ronald to look at you," Walter ordered.

"Hi there!" Charlie waved his hands to get Ronald's attention.

Ronald ignored the gesture. Charlie shouted louder, and the Agent's eyes rested on him apprehensively. He didn't say anything, but turned to see whom Charlie was waving at.

"Ronald Logan," Walter said. "That is your name, isn't it?"

"Who said that?" Ronald whirled around with his hands poised to strike.

"You and your brothers died in your sleep," Walter continued. "Of smoke inhalation."

Ronald muttered another incantation, causing a surge of purple light to crackle at his fingertips. "Show yourself, demon!"

"I'm standing right in front of you, but I'm guessing you really wouldn't recognize me, since we barely met less than a week ago," Walter said.

Ronald turned and looked once again at Charlie. His eyes narrowed with suspicion. "Is that you? Can you see me?"

Charlie wore a goofy smile and nodded. "Yeah, I can see you, but I'm not the one talking." He pointed at his chest, whispering, "He's inside me."

Ronald's right eye twitched. "*Inside* you?" The small orb of light began to pulsate. "Were those shades with *you*?"

"No—I mean ... I guess they were following us, but they're not *with* us." Charlie held up his hands. "They were trying to attack us. That's why we're here. We need your help!"

" 'We'? Who's 'we'?" Ronald demanded.

"You're not going to believe this," Walter said proudly. "But it's me, Walter Prairie."

Ronald swallowed and scrunched his nose in confusion. "Who?"

"Walter Prairie. Don't you remember? It was, like, just last week. I was standing in front of Alton's desk, and you and your brothers walked by."

"Look, I'm sorry, but I have no clue—"

"Struck by lightning." Walter deliberately said it slowly, drawing out the words.

This time Ronald's eyes brightened, and his mouth dropped open wider. "The new kid? Walter?"

"In the flesh," Walter answered. "Well, not *my* flesh."

"But how? You were just getting ready to enlist in the Academy. How are you here? And who's *this* kid?" He gestured to Charlie. "What are you doing inside him?"

"I'll explain everything, but we need to talk, and I really need your help. Is it okay if you hang out with us and leave your target alone for a bit?"

Ronald glanced at the house. "Are you sure those shades were following you?"

Charlie nodded quickly.

"Yeah, I guess they would have to be. This place is as boring as school. My assignment is pretty lame. Come on. I'll take you to the park down the road. That should give us some privacy."

30

B. & O. Railroad

A rotund demon covered in coarse blue fur stood in the doorway of Hoonga's office, timidly clutching a crumpled piece of paper. "Thought you'd want to know."

Hoonga's lower lip bent into a menacing curl. "Are you sure they were the ones I sent, Paraput?"

The blue demon nodded as he glanced once more at the paper, trembling in his flabby paws. "Shades two-forty-two and two-sixty-seven, master. They were exterminated just now by a Celestial burst."

Hoonga scowled down at the floor to where Trutti stood looking as innocent as possible. "Trutti? I thought I told you they were not to be spotted."

Trutti shrugged, but took a cautious step away from his master's leg. "Don't look at *me*. I told the shades what to do. I was very specific."

Hoonga slapped his forehead in frustration. "Clearly, you weren't as specific as— Wait!" The Cyclops's brow furrowed as he looked once more at the messenger in the doorway. "You said they were exterminated by a Celestial burst? How is that possible? I was told Charlie's Agent doesn't have the ability to create bursts."

"I—I—don't know. I just read the report, sir. I'm sorry." The blue demon lumbered as fast as he could away from the office as Hoonga slammed the door behind him.

The report could have been a mistake, but Hoonga knew in his heart that Paraput's reports were rarely wrong. Which meant that Walter, Charlie's meddlesome Agent, had somehow discovered a way to conjure Celestial energy. This was not good. Not good at all.

"Argh! I'm surrounded by *idiots!*" Hoonga shouted. For all he knew, Charlie and Walter were discovering the way to destroy *The Summoner's Handbook,* and Hoonga was running out of employees to send to take it from them.

Hoonga paused briefly at the refrigerator to remove a mason jar sloshing with putrid yellow liquid before returning to his desk and dropping into his chair.

Trutti's sharp claws clacked against the floor as he scurried over and poked his bat ears above the desk. "Master? Are you mad at me?"

Tipping the mason jar back, Hoonga downed half the contents before gasping for air. "Mad at you? Why would I be mad at you? Unless you didn't do what you were supposed to do. In that case, I would be very—"

"I did everything I was supposed to do," Trutti interjected. "I've been spying on the boy at his home and at his school. And I told those shades what was expected. They just didn't listen."

Hoonga belched and wiped the liquid dripping from his lips. "They never do, do they?"

"Stupid. Every last one of them," Trutti agreed. "I've always said your entire legion of shades share one teensy brain, and that only works half the time."

Hoonga cracked a smile, but it didn't remain long. He had too many things to worry about now. The Underworld was becoming a complicated place. Gone were the days of simple demonic mayhem. Yes, finding *The Summoner's Handbook* and opening the Gateway would make life more interesting, but how much fun would it really be having to listen to that man with the enormous Celestial stone barking out orders? There would always be someone else in charge.

Trutti tilted his head as he stared at his master. Then his eyes widened with delight. "I almost forgot!" Racing across the room, Trutti leapt over his pile of moldy blankets and undid the latches of his leather suitcase. Hoonga watched with curiosity as the lesser demon rummaged around. He raised his eyebrow in surprise when Trutti returned carrying a flat box and dumped several red and green cubes onto Hoonga's desk, along with hundreds of colorful small sheets of paper.

"It's called Mo-nop-o-ly," Trutti explained, swiveling his head to read the upside-down title. "I took a risk and lifted it during one of my most recent scouting assignments. Thought I would surprise you."

Grinning, Hoonga sniffed one of the silvery game pieces, in the shape of an old shoe. "Pewter. How clever! Oh, look! Fashioned in the shape of tiny houses!" There was no masking his glee as he plucked up one of the green squares and showed it to Trutti. "How is it played?"

Trutti folded his arms. "I don't know, but I think there are instructions. It looks disgusting, if you ask me."

Hoonga chuckled and stroked Trutti's ears with his clawed finger. "I know how much it must have bothered you to carry this all the way back to the Underworld. Thank you, my friend."

Dutifully puffing out his chest, Trutti closed his eyes. "You can torture me with it, if you'd like. For messing up with the shades. I suppose I wasn't clear enough with my instructions to them, and I deserve to be punished."

Hoonga clucked his tongue. "No, no. That won't be necessary."

"I insist! I need to redeem myself to you, master."

A blaring clatter erupted from the telephone resting on the corner of Hoonga's desk.

"Why must I always be interrupted, just when I'm about to have some fun?" But Hoonga picked up the receiver with a look of concern in his eye and placed it to his ear.

"You will come to the rendezvous point tonight," the voice hissed on the other end of the line.

"How did you get this number?" Hoonga snarled.

"You fool. Have you forgotten who I work for? I have infinite resources at my disposal. The time of sitting around and waiting is over. It must happen *tonight!*"

"We don't have the boy yet—or the book."

"I know that!" the voice snapped. "There's going to be a storm late tonight. It's the perfect condition for the Gateway to be opened. You need to bring Charlie to me."

"But how? Even with the storm, I just can't manifest in the boy's home uninvited. That's not how it works. I'm not some puny lesser demon"—Hoonga covered the receiver with his hand and whispered "Sorry, Trutti" before continuing—"I have too much dark mass. You'll have to be there to make the invitation."

The voice groaned on the other end. "I can't! I'm . . . involved in other things. Things that I just can't step away from to do *your* job. I knew I should've gone with my other choice from the beginning. You've done nothing but fail!"

Hoonga's eyelid narrowed as he twirled one of the Monopoly game pieces between his thumb and forefinger. "Regardless of your insults, the fact remains that greater demons are unable to enter human abodes without a demonic summoning. Since you're not willing to take a break from your *busy* schedule"—he winked at Trutti—"I guess that still leaves us with a bit of a problem."

There was silence on the other end, and Hoonga waited patiently for his instruction. The Cyclops held up a card from the box to show to Trutti and smiled as he mouthed the words "B.O. Railroad." Trutti scratched his ear, not understanding his master's humor.

"Very well," the voice returned. "This is what you are to do. Gather up all of your followers, and meet me at the rendezvous point the moment the first raindrop falls."

"What about Charlie?" Hoonga asked.

"Keep the boy and the book contained in his apartment until we are ready to make a strike. Do you have something capable of handling that assignment?"

Hoonga thought about the request and glanced at Trutti. "I think so," he said, half nodding.

"I seriously doubt that!" he spat, and hung up.

Hoonga returned the receiver to its cradle. Eagerly wiggling his fingers, he laid out the Monopoly game board on his desk and lined up the pewter pieces in the square marked with the big red "Go" and an arrow.

Trutti kept his distance, gagging and sticking out his tongue as his master stacked the colorful sheets of paper into neat piles.

"Trutti?" Hoonga asked once the game board was set. "I think I'll reconsider your offer of redeeming yourself."

Trutti's shoulders drooped. "Of course," he whimpered. "I'll play as much as you like."

"Oh no. I wasn't meaning the game. I need Charlie to stay put in his apartment. He can't escape until we spring our trap. Could you do that?"

Trutti's ears perked up. "Absolutely! Who shall I have to command? Give me some wraiths instead of shades. Sepa and Deander? They're my favorites. They tell the best ghost stories."

Hoonga frowned. "I'm afraid you're going to have to do this alone. I need every able-bodied demon at the rendezvous point."

"Alone?" Trutti gulped. "But how? He has an Afterlife Academy Agent who's able to shoot Celestial beams! I could disintegrate!"

"Now, now, don't be so grim. You're not to engage, you just need to keep Charlie inside his apartment. This is a great

opportunity for you to prove your worth and use your resources. I'm sure you'll think of something. Until then, we
have a little time on our hands. I'll even let you go first."
Hoonga's eye twinkled with excitement as he slid a pair of
dice toward Trutti.

Pieces of the Puzzle

R onald ogled Charlie's face in disbelief as he sat beneath
a large tree in a family park, staring at the front cover of
The Summoner's Handbook.

"Could you please stop looking at me like that?" Charlie
begged.

"Sorry, man. I keep forgetting you can see me." Ronald
sat back, giving Charlie space.

"But you can't see *me*," Walter said. "Why not?"

"Because you're inside Charlie. That's how a possession
works. At least, that's what they told us at the Academy. I still
can't believe you possessed him!"

"It was an accident," Walter said. "All I was trying to do
was not screw up on my first day."

Walter had gone over almost everything that had happened. His abrupt assignment in the field without training.
The shades and the banshee in Charlie's room. *The Summoner's Handbook.* The demon attack out on Charlie's street.

"But still, possession is, like, majorly difficult to do. Some Agents never master it, even after years of training."

"Well, I'm not one to brag, but—"

"I hate to break it to you, but you've got a real problem," Ronald interrupted. "Possession is a last resort. Every Agent knows that."

"Could we talk about the book now?" Charlie piped up. They were completely alone in the park.

Ronald nodded. "Open it for me."

Charlie carefully peeled back the cover and started flipping through. Occasionally, a detailed image of a demon would appear on one of the pages, and Charlie would pause to allow Ronald time to examine it.

After a couple of minutes, Ronald released a frustrated sigh. "I don't understand any of it. You can read it?" he asked.

"Yes," Charlie answered, not looking directly at the pages. "But only because I read this page." He hurriedly turned to the back to show Ronald the special page. "Once you stare at this long enough, you can read everything else."

Ronald stared at the page, concentrating. "How long do I have to look at it?"

"Don't bother," Walter said. "I tried, but it was no use."

"Yeah, and he's a 'natural.'" Charlie made quotation marks with his fingers.

Ronald blinked his eyes rapidly, looked away, then looked back at the page. "It's not working. How do you even know it's *The Summoner's Handbook*?"

"It's written by Igor Yad," Walter explained.

Ronald sighed. "Yeah, that name does sound familiar from one of my training classes."

"Besides, why else would there be demons and shades and everything else attacking us?" Charlie asked.

"Well, what do your parents do for a living?" Ronald asked.

"We've already gone over this. His dad's a driver for Carmichael," Walter said.

"What about his mom?"

"She . . . ," Walter started, but hesitated. "Uh, Charlie, what does she do?"

"She scrapbooks," Charlie answered.

"It sounds to me like there's no reason why you should have been assigned as an HLT," Ronald said.

"A what?" Charlie asked.

"A High-Level Target. Take my HLT, for example. Tyrone Underhill." Ronald whipped out his laminated card with Tyrone's information. "He's popular, wealthy, and quite the athlete. He's also a real jerk to people for no reason at all."

"Sounds like a lot of people I know," Charlie said.

"Yeah. No biggie, right? Well, according to his sleep patterns, on more than one occasion, Tyrone has dreamed of being a bank robber."

"Yikes," Walter said.

"Tell me about it." Ronald folded his arms. "Now, throw in the fact that Tyrone's dad is the CEO of Carmichael Armored Vehicles. That's a disaster waiting to happen. Demons gobble that sort of stuff up, which makes Tyrone a High-Level Target."

"Thanks for sharing, but what does this have to do with me?" Charlie asked.

"If your parents aren't doing anything dangerous, and

you aren't having dangerous thoughts, that would mean the only reason you'd be labeled as an HLT was that you really did find *The Summoner's Handbook.*"

"That's what we've been saying!" Walter said. "Now can you see how big this is?"

"But that's what doesn't make sense to me." Ronald stood up. "If this is the book—*the* book—the one all the creatures of the Underworld are looking for in order to wreak havoc on the earth—then, no offense, Walter, but why did the Academy send *you*?"

"I suppose you could do a better job?"

"I wouldn't go jumping straight to possession on my first day, if that's what you mean. But Charlie should have a whole squadron of Agents surrounding him at all times. The best of the best. The Afterlife Academy soldiers used for generals and presidents and nuclear physicists should be at his disposal until *The Summoner's Handbook* is either safely hidden or destroyed. Instead they just sent *you*. The newest member of the Academy. Untrained. No experience. What weapons did they give you?"

"Weapons? None." Walter sounded deflated.

Ronald raised his eyebrows. "What about resource manuals? Training guides?"

"Darwin gave me a pamphlet."

"Let me see it," Ronald said.

"It's in my pocket. I can't exactly reach it from where I'm sitting."

Ronald groaned. "What pocket did you stick it in?"

"My right one."

Ronald drew near to Charlie, who immediately scampered backward on the ground. "Um, what do you think you're doing?"

"Relax." In one quick motion, Ronald shot his hand into Charlie's front pocket and pulled out the folded ready-reference guide.

"How did you—" Walter started to ask, but Ronald's agitated voice shot him down.

"This is it? This is all he gave you? This is pointless!" He wadded up the pamphlet and chucked it toward the swings on the playground. "So he didn't give you any of this equipment?" Unsnapping one of the compartments on his utility belt, Ronald produced three small trinkets.

"What *is* that stuff?" Charlie asked.

Ronald held up a square black contraption resembling a small cell phone. "This is an ETD, an Energy Transfer Device. Agents use it to harness their energy with their target's energy in order to ward off large attacks from wraiths, Dark Omens, and demons. This is the safest way to gain the advantage over the enemy. But since you've jumped to the last chapter of the training manual and decided to *possess* Charlie, you wouldn't have any use for an ETD." Next, Ronald held up a small whistle and handed it to Charlie. "It's called a Feral Whistle, and it works with animals."

"I can't hold it, can I?" Charlie looked at the whistle and then back at Ronald.

"Let's see," Ronald said. "Walter, when I drop it, I want you to try to hold it as well."

Charlie opened his hand, and Ronald dropped the

whistle. Instead of passing through his skin, as Charlie assumed would happen, the whistle rested on his palm. He closed his fingers over its cold surface and smiled.

"To do what you two just did, I would have to use the ETD. And that's the problem. Something has changed you, Charlie, and your ability to interact with spirits. Demons and wraiths typically can't touch a human. All they can do is whisper temptations, scare them, and try to possess them. Unless the conditions are altered in the right way. If that happens, demons can physically attack a human."

"What sorts of things could alter the conditions?" Walter asked.

"Oh, I don't know. Like possessing your HLT or meddling with things you shouldn't?" Ronald pointed to the book.

"Are you saying a demon can attack me now?" Charlie whispered. "Because I read this thing? They haven't really hurt me yet—just Walter."

"The ability of demons to hurt you will increase the longer you're possessed," Ronald explained. "Possession protects an HLT at first, but it's only supposed to be used for short amounts of time. By reading the book, you've opened yourself up to a whole new world. It's the one my brothers and I live in now. The one Walter lives in."

"You said this whistle works with animals? Why would you need to use it?" Walter asked.

"Animals have weaker wills than humans, so demons use them from time to time to attack an HLT. If you're lucky, blowing on the Feral Whistle can snap an animal out of a trance. Or, it can be used to control animals for an Agent's benefit. But it depends on the animal and how deep a trance it's been put under."

Charlie pointed to the last item in Ronald's hand. "What's that other thing do?"

"This"—Ronald held up a shard of what looked like purple glass—"is a piece of Celestial stone. Every Agent is assigned a piece. I'd let you touch it if I could, but it would explode."

"Explode?" Walter and Charlie asked together.

"It only works when the Agent assigned to it uses it. If another Agent or something else takes hold of it, the stone's rigged to blow up. It has some sort of internal self-destruct button." The shard of Celestial stone glittered in the sunlight. Charlie could feel energy emanating from it. "Do you remember the shield of light I made earlier to protect Tyrone? And the bolt I shot at the shades? If I didn't have this, I couldn't have done that. Celestial stones are very powerful. But a piece this small can do only so much. It can destroy up to four shades at a time without any difficulty. A weaker wraith or two, no problem. If you get attacked by a Dark Omen or a demon, nuh-uh. Not a chance. I don't need any more than this, because I'll probably never see anything bigger than a wraith while guarding Tyrone. You should've been given a brick of Celestial stone." Ronald returned the items to his pouch.

"Why didn't they give *you* any of this cool stuff?" Charlie asked Walter.

"Who knows? I think there's something fishy going on."

"It's obviously the demon leader," Charlie said.

Ronald bit his lip. "I'm not even sure there *is* one leader.

Demons hate rules and order. Things are a bit chaotic down there. Even if there were one leader, I don't think he'd be able to organize and activate the rest to get the book. And anyway, he'd need a nondemon to help summon an army of demons."

"What nondemon would want to do that?" asked Charlie.

"Someone who's unhappy with the way things are."

"Well, that could be anyone on earth," Walter said.

"I'm not thinking about people on earth," Ronald responded.

"Huh?" Charlie and Walter intoned in unison.

"I'm thinking it has to be someone at the Afterlife Academy. Someone who's unhappy but doesn't have enough power to change things from within."

Walter and Ronald spoke at the same time: "Alton."

"Who?" said Charlie.

"Alton's a Categorizer," Ronald explained. "He's not really in the Academy, but he has access to a lot of Academy information, especially about the members he's Categorized. Who knows what he's learned over the years. He's been there forever."

Walter added, "He's the guy who gave and graded the assessment I got the perfect score on—the one that showed I didn't need any training before becoming an Afterlife Academy Agent. He's not the chirpiest guy. Still, it's hard to believe—"

"Yeah, but you don't know the whole story. When Alton died, he tried to enroll at the Academy but was turned down. Instead, he was assigned to Janitorial Services." Ronald stuck out his tongue. "Cleaning toilets."

Charlie scrunched his nose. "You guys need toilets?"

"He did that for a long time, but finally made it into Categorizing," Ronald continued, ignoring Charlie's question. "Over the years, Alton has applied to dozens of positions at the Academy, but the board rejects him every time. Apparently, they don't think he has what it takes to be an Agent."

"The board?" Charlie said.

"The Board of Directors. They make all the big decisions at the Academy. Who gets in. Who's rejected. Who gets assigned to world calamities. All that stuff."

"You think Alton could be doing this to get back at the board for not letting him into the Academy?" Walter asked.

"I guess, if he's bitter enough. He always just seemed grumpy to me. But he *has* been Categorizing a long time now, and he probably knows a loophole or two in the system."

"That has to be it," Charlie announced. "Alton must have altered Walter's answers and tricked the board into thinking he was so much more than some regular kid. Why else would they have let us wander around without any protection?"

"Hey! I've protected you some. And who's to say I *didn't* get all the answers right?"

"I'll check on Tyrone, make sure he's secure," Ronald said. "Then I'll head back up to the Academy to do some digging."

"You can do that?" Walter asked. "Just go back up there whenever you want?"

Ronald growled in frustration. "Were you not set up with an Access Portal?"

"Probably not," Walter answered pathetically. "Who's in charge of doing that?"

"I don't know where they come from, but Alton was the person who gave me mine."

"I remember!" Walter raised his voice. "That little paper-clip thingy on your belt."

"All right. I'm going to get to the bottom of this. In the meantime, don't go outside at night. There's bound to be more wraiths or other things out there waiting for you. Plus, there's going to be a rainstorm late tonight, so do your best to stay hidden and out of sight."

"What's so bad about rain?" Walter asked.

"The changes in the atmosphere from a rainstorm allow demons to come out of their underground hiding places."

"We *have* had trouble mainly when it's been raining!"

"Yeah, and tonight's storm is going to spread across two or three states. It's a big one. That means the demons will be much stronger, and you can't take any risks, especially now, since they can attack Charlie."

"Hey, I'm looking out for the little guy," Walter said.

"Little guy?"

"You need to be careful too, Walter," Ronald added. "Demons don't just hurt your essence when they touch you, they can destroy you completely."

"But wouldn't I just end up back in a Categorizing Office?"

"Not for a very long time. You'd spend eons in a place neither here nor there. Your spirit would need to be rebuilt, and that takes loads of time. It's not a fun way to go." Ronald pulled out a small pad of paper and a pencil from his utility belt and scribbled a message. "Here, take this." He held out the paper, and Charlie, with Walter's help, closed his fingers around it.

rlogan36@afterlifeacademy.hvn

"You have an email address?" Charlie asked.

Ronald nodded. "The Internet is just waves of communication. Agents can use it too. We all have accounts. Email me if you get in a jam, and I'll send help. Otherwise, I'll plan on meeting up with you guys once I find out what's going on."

Charlie stuck the note in his pocket, then held out the Feral Whistle to Ronald.

"Keep it," Ronald said. "It could come in handy."

Another Crumpled Letter

A lton stared down at the white envelope in his hands. It was different from the other envelopes stacked on his desk, the ones containing Categorizing information on the new arrivals. This one was addressed directly to Alton and bore the Afterlife Academy crest stamped at the center of the envelope. Alton ran his thumb under the flap and pulled out the letter. He held his breath and scrunched up his face in stern concentration as he read.

Dear Alton Tremonton:

We the members of the Board of Directors appreciate your recent application to the position of Team Leader. As you are well aware, this is an exceptionally difficult position to fill. There are many supremely qualified applicants interested in joining the Academy leadership. It is with regret that we must respectfully reject your

*application, as we have selected a different candidate,
one who has the precise qualifications and experience
we are looking for at the Academy. Please don't let this
discourage you. There will be future opportunities.*

Another rejection. Alton's nostrils flared as he glanced at
the bottom of the letter, where Darwin Pollock's fancy signa-
ture took up a quarter of the page.

"Pulled some strings, did you?" Alton grumbled. He
ripped open his bottom desk drawer and tossed the rejection
letter in with the others, all signed by Darwin.

"He thinks I'm a fool. That I'm incapable. That I don't
know what's going on here."

"What *is* going on here?" a girl asked from one of the
chairs across the room. The chair had been empty just moments before, and the girl looked around the office in utter
confusion.

"Name and age!" Alton snapped. "Make it quick, and
don't trifle with me, young lady. I'm not in the mood."

The girl blinked, but complied.

"I'll show Darwin," Alton muttered under his breath as
he fished the girl's file from the tower of folders. He removed
his glasses and wiped a smudge from one of the lenses. "I'll
show them all who the real fool is."

Cracking the Whip

Charlie hadn't realized how late it had gotten. When the transit bus dropped him off at the stop nearest his street, the sun had already begun to set, leaving a pink pool of sky overhead.

"I'm so dead!" He raced up the street toward his apartment.

"What is it?" Walter demanded. "Get low! Hide somewhere! What do you see? Is it a demon? A wraith?"

"It's my parents," Charlie said.

"What's wrong with them? I don't see them!"

"They're gonna kill me! Do you know what time it is? I have a strict curfew!"

Charlie didn't participate in any after-school activities. No sports, no extracurricular clubs, like German or chess. Unlike Walter, Charlie had never gotten a detention and had always arrived home promptly just before three-thirty. He should've been home from school three and a half hours ago. How was he going to explain the gap of time?

"No offense, but your parents are the least of our worries right now," Walter said.

"Easy for you to say." Charlie bounded up the steps of the apartment three at a time. "You're not the one they're gonna mutilate."

A police officer was standing outside the apartment door jotting down information on a notepad when Charlie reached the top of the stairs. He was going to be grounded until Christmas.

"Mrs. Dewdle, is this him?" the police officer asked through the opening in the doorway.

Charlie's mom's tear-streaked face appeared beside the officer. She raced down the hallway and enveloped Charlie in a bone-crunching hug.

"Are you hurt?" she asked, examining him for injuries. Charlie quickly shook his head. "Where have you been?" Her growl sounded almost demonic.

"Mom, it's—I can explain."

Mr. Dewdle shook the officer's hand, thanked him, and pointed a shaky finger into the apartment. "Get inside, and sit down!"

With Mrs. Dewdle's fingers digging into his shoulder, Charlie was escorted past the police officer and through the door.

"You're so dead," Charlie's little sister, Darcy, whispered in Charlie's ear as he sat in one of the wingback chairs in the living room. His parents were standing in the kitchen, discussing the proper punishment. Darcy was relishing every minute of it. "Mom called all the neighbors. She called the school. And then she called the police."

"Get out of here, Darcy!" Charlie hissed.

"*So* grounded!" Darcy smiled and folded her arms.

"She's adorable," Walter muttered. "How old is she?"

"She's seven," Charlie answered.

Darcy blinked, her smile faltering. "Huh?"

"I just said you were seven."

Darcy looked around the room. "To who?"

"To my friend Walter." Now it was Charlie's turn to fold his arms. "He's a ghost, and he's in the room right now, looking at you."

Walter laughed. "That's hilarious! Look at her face!"

"Stop it!" Her hands fell into her lap. "You're lying. Stop trying to scare me."

Charlie grinned. "I'm not lying. Am I, Walter?" The uneasy silence in the room was all it took to set her squirming.

"*Mom!*" Darcy jumped off the couch, retreated down the hallway, and slammed her bedroom door.

"Now you've done it," Walter said, still laughing.

"I don't care." Charlie stared down at the floor.

Both Charlie's parents sat down on the couch across from him, their expressions solemn. "I spoke to the assistant principal this afternoon," Charlie's mom started. "He says you didn't show up for your last two classes today, and others this week. Is that true?"

Charlie managed to shrug.

"That doesn't sound like you," she said. "Since when did you start skipping school?"

Charlie didn't know how to explain any of what had been going on lately. It wasn't like they would believe him anyway. He glanced up from the floor. His parents did not look happy.

"So you just skipped school for no reason?" his dad asked.

"No." Charlie opted to offer only one-word answers until he could devise an appropriate alibi, but his mind was drawing a blank.

"I know you're doing an amazing job explaining things to them, but maybe you should try telling them what's really going on." Walter's voice broke the temporary silence.

Tell them the truth? He couldn't do that.

"Your sister tells us she's heard you talking to yourself lately. Is there something you want to tell us? Do you have some sort of imaginary friend?" his mom asked meekly.

How old did she think he was?

Mr. Dewdle rolled his eyes. "Imaginary friend? Don't be ridiculous, Dana."

"It's perfectly normal, Martin. Children have imaginary friends," she said.

"Four-year-olds have imaginary friends," his dad snapped. "You're not four, are you, son?"

Something thudded against the apartment door.

Charlie's dad stood. "What was that?"

"It sounded like someone knocking," Charlie's mom said.

"Are you expecting somebody?" his dad asked.

She shook her head. "No, but it could be the police stopping by with follow-up questions."

Mr. Dewdle walked to the door and opened it, and Charlie peered over the couch for a better view. His dad stepped through the opening, looked in either direction, and scratched his chin. "You heard the knock, right?"

Charlie's mom turned toward the door. "Is someone playing a prank?"

Charlie stood up. He had a really bad feeling. Who would doorbell-ditch an apartment on the third floor? They had all heard the knock. So where had the knocker gone?

"Are you thinking what I'm thinking?" Walter asked. Charlie nodded slowly. "I knew there'd be trouble."

As Charlie's dad pulled the door shut behind him, something small and brown shot through the opening.

Charlie yelped and hopped up on the chair.

"What is it?" his mom asked, also rising to her feet.

Nipping at Mr. Dewdle's feet stood a miniature cocker spaniel with floppy brown ears. "Where did you come from?"

"Is that a dog?" Charlie's mom asked.

"Looks like it."

"Well, get it out before it wets the carpet! Oh, Martin, I just had it cleaned!"

"I'm trying, dear, but he's pretty mad. Maybe he's rabid."

The dog's head pivoted like an owl's until its glassy eyes focused on Charlie. With a new target in sight, it charged around the couch and leapt onto the coffee table. Charlie's parents snatched the couch pillows in their hands, trying to corner the dog, but it kept its focus on Charlie.

"You've got to get rid of your dumb birds, Charlie!" Walter shouted.

"Dogs don't normally just charge into apartments," Charlie fired back. Then he noticed something unusual about the canine. "Look at its eyes!"

"I see them!"

The cocker spaniel's eyes were like two hollow marbles, but instead of black pupils, it had faint reddish lights dilating in its eye sockets.

"What about them?" his father asked.

"You think it's—" Charlie whimpered to Walter.

"Get the whistle!" Walter ordered.

Charlie crammed his fingers in his pocket, and with Walter's help, pulled out the whistle. Placing the small instrument in his mouth, Charlie pressed down with his lips and blew. A sharp sound pierced the air, and the dog barked in reply. The red color in its eyes faded, and a panting tongue replaced the previous snarl. The dog began to wag its tail and bowed when Mr. Dewdle reached down to pick him up.

Mrs. Dewdle ran and filled a bowl with water, and the dog drank thirstily.

"Well, that was bizarre, wasn't it, now?" Charlie's dad laughed.

Charlie and Walter knew the dog's behavior was no laughing matter.

"Where do you think it came from? Do any of your neighbors own pets?" Walter asked.

"I don't think so," Charlie answered.

"You don't think that was bizarre?" asked Charlie's dad. "It doesn't get much stranger than that."

Having drunk its fill, the dog trotted around and began to paw at the door.

"It's probably from across the street," Mrs. Dewdle said. "Charlie, why don't you take it to the vet and see if they're missing one of their dogs?"

"Why me?"

Both of his parents glared at him.

Charlie bent down and cradled the dog in his arms. It sniffed him, then looked away with a disgusted expression.

"I don't think you should go outside," Walter said. "What if that wraith is there?"

Charlie glanced back at his parents. "It's not like I have a choice." Slowly pulling open the apartment door, he peered out into the hall.

Walter screamed first.

Charlie joined him shortly after.

At least two dozen snarling dogs of various sizes poured into the hallway from the stairs. Even from this distance, Charlie could see the red glow in their eyes as drool dripped from their mouths. Behind the dogs, coercing them forward with a black whip, stood a gray bat-eared demon grinning wildly. All at once, the dogs released a bone-chilling howl and charged.

Duped

"Yes, Frederick, what is it?" Darwin looked up as his assistant stepped into the office.

"Apologies, sir, for the interruption. There's an Agent here to see you," Frederick announced.

"Did I miss an appointment?" Darwin scratched the side of his mouth with his finger, glancing at his planner.

"No, sir. But he says it's urgent. He came straight from the field."

Darwin leaned forward. "Who is it?" he whispered.

"Ronald Logan."

Darwin mouthed the name twice, shaking his head. Then his eyes widened a bit. "Ah, yes, one of the three Logan brothers." He examined his pocket watch. "I have that meeting to attend, as you know, so this will have to be brief. Do send him in."

Frederick exited the office, and when the door reopened, Ronald Logan entered.

"Hello there, Ronald, my boy. Please, have a seat." Darwin smiled and motioned toward the chair in front of his desk.

"Thank you, Mr. Pollock." Ronald sat down. "I'm sorry for not making an appointment. I didn't have much time."

"That's all right. I am in a bit of a hurry, but I always have time for my young Agents. Now, what is this urgent matter you have to discuss?"

"I think someone has found *The Summoner's Handbook*."

"*The Summoner's Handbook*?" Darwin pressed the tips of his fingers together. "Why do you think this?"

"Because I've seen it, sir. With my own eyes."

"Your HLT has come into possession of this book?"

"Not mine. Walter Prairie's."

Darwin opened his mouth, but didn't speak. He looked once more at his pocket watch. "Walter Prairie," he said.

"He's in over his head. He doesn't know what he's doing, and he and Charlie—"

"Charlie?" Darwin chimed in.

"Walter's HLT," Ronald explained. "They don't stand a chance against a horde of demons."

"I think you must be exaggerating, son. I find it hard to believe that something as potentially dangerous as *The Summoner's Handbook* could have gone under our radar like that."

"I'm not exaggerating. And Walter and I think there's more going on too."

"Like what?"

"We think someone up here is trying to help the demons."

"Here? That's preposterous! I know you're only trying to help, but you are a new Agent. Do you understand what you're implying? Corruption. Deceit. In the Afterlife Academy! Those are serious allegations." Darwin spoke with the patience of wisdom and experience.

Ronald shrank down in his seat. "Not necessarily the Academy, sir. Just someone with access. Like Alton."

Darwin's brow crinkled, and he showed real concern for the first time. "Alton? Alton Tremonton? Ronald, think about what you're saying. You are suggesting that a Categorizer, a dutiful employee of thirty years, has cruelly and purposefully duped the entire Board of Directors, has somehow made contact with a demon horde, and is orchestrating an attack on an Academy Agent and his target?"

Ronald chewed on his lip. "Well, yeah. Maybe."

"Mr. Logan, you are an Afterlife Academy Agent. You are assigned to protect an individual. But you are also assigned, at all times, to uphold the standards of this Academy. You are implicating a loyal employee without providing me with any proof. I know you mean well, but you would do well to incorporate some loyalty and trust into your sense of duty, along with your curiosity and ambitious drive, both of which are qualities I admire as well. Do you understand?"

"Yes, sir. I'm sorry, sir."

"Don't apologize, young Ronald. You were trying to do what is right, and you make me and the Academy proud in so doing. Now, you had better return to your HLT. You don't want to abandon your first post."

"No, sir." Ronald got up and walked toward the door.

But he turned around to ask one more question. "Sir, if you don't mind my asking, how did Walter Prairie bypass the Academy?"

"Ah, Walter Prairie. I was informed that he was a special young man. I suspect that is quite true. He is more powerful than we think."

"Yes, sir."

Once Ronald had disappeared from the office and the door had closed, Darwin buried his face in his hands.

"Alton Tremonton. It would appear I'm the one who's been duped."

No More Talk of Spirits

Still holding the cocker spaniel, Charlie hopped back into the apartment and slammed the door as the first wave of dogs arrived.

"Get back!" he ordered as a heavy weight smashed against the door. The old wood creaked from the strain. The cocker spaniel scampered free from Charlie's grip and darted under the couch.

"What is that?" his mom demanded.

"*Dogs!*" Charlie shouted. "Lots and lots of dogs!"

Another crash, and the sound of splintering wood as the dogs pile-drove themselves against the door. It wouldn't hold much longer.

"We've got to send out a message for help!" Walter said. "Get to the computer!"

Charlie grabbed the hands of his bewildered parents and yanked them toward the hallway, pausing only for a second to pluck his backpack with *The Summoner's Handbook* from the chair. Darcy stood just outside her bedroom door, screaming as her father scooped her up in his arms and followed Charlie into the study.

"Not in here!" Mr. Dewdle grabbed Charlie's sleeve. "There's not enough room!"

But it was too late to pick a different hideout. From out in the living room, the apartment door imploded, and scores of ravenous dogs, entranced by the bat-eared demon, scrambled over one another to get to Charlie.

Charlie's mom locked the door, and his dad propped the top of the desk chair under the doorknob to secure it.

"What's the matter, Charlie? Are you choking?" his mom asked.

Charlie couldn't answer because he was too busy blowing violently on the Feral Whistle, invisible to his parents. But the dogs kept hammering against the door.

"It's not working!" Charlie spat the whistle out in his hand.

"There's probably too many of them," Walter said.

"You're right, that door's not going to keep them out!" Mr. Dewdle said in response to Charlie's response to Walter. Charlie's flock of caged birds filled the air with agitated screeching.

"How are we supposed to concentrate with all that ruckus?" Walter hollered, trying to drown out their squawks.

Charlie managed to quell the birds with several handfuls of bird feed and then turned his attention to the computer desk.

"Martin, why are all those dogs out there?" Mrs. Dewdle asked. "Do you think someone let them out?"

"Not someone . . . some*thing*." Charlie clicked on the computer and tapped his hand anxiously as he waited for the system to boot up. It was time to come clean.

"What are you talking about?"

"Mom, Dad," Charlie said, his chest heaving, "there's something you need to know about me." He clicked on the Internet icon and navigated to his email account.

Charlie's sister covered her ears with her hands as the dogs started tearing at the study door. Charlie knew they had only minutes before the dogs found a way to break through.

"Those dogs are being controlled by a monster. I think it's a demon. Though it's not raining, which doesn't make any sense, but I don't really have time to think it through."

"Dana, what is he talking about?"

Walter dictated as Charlie typed a message to Ronald Logan's email.

Ronald,

We are trapped in the apartment! Dogs are everywhere, and they want to eat us. Send help fast!

Charlie and Walter

Charlie's dad read through the message before Charlie could send it. "Who's Ronald? Who's Walter?"

Taking a deep breath, Charlie began to explain. "Walter is a Guardian Agent sent to help me. He's kind of like a guardian angel." He swallowed. "He's inside me."

Charlie's mother groaned in exasperation. "Not this again, Charlie. Haven't we already been through this? These games you play. They're not healthy."

"It's not a game, Mom! A few days ago, I found *The Summoner's Handbook,* and now all heck is breaking loose. Every demon wants it, and I don't know how to get rid of it. That's why I was late today. I went to Pressley so Walter could talk to Ronald Logan, another Agent. And now we think there may be some sort of conspiracy happening. Though we don't know exactly what kind of conspiracy just yet." It all made perfect sense in Charlie's mind, but by the haggard looks on his parents' faces and by Walter's soft chuckling in his ear, it was clear that Charlie was failing to deliver the point.

"I see." Mr. Dewdle dug at the corners of his eyes with his thumbs.

Charlie clacked in another web address, and he cheered when he saw a message from Wisdom Willows in his SpiritSpy.org in-box. "He wrote me!"

"What are you doing now?" his dad demanded. "We need to get out of this room, and then we need to get your head checked by a doctor."

"Dad, there's nothing wrong with my head. I'm telling you the truth. Now please be quiet while I read this." Both his parents' mouths clamped shut in surprise. Several dog claws began scratching at the opening beneath the door.

```
Charlie,

Hope all is well. Good news! There is
a way to properly dispose of The Sum-
```

moner's Handbook. It took me a while to
find out, but it should be easy enough
to do. You'll need to burn it using a
Chamber Torch. If you have access to a
cemetery with underground tombs, you
should be able to find one. If not, I
happen to own a couple of torches, but
I'm out of town until next week. I'm
attending the Wraith Festival in Conrad, Minnesota. Any way you could get
here? We can destroy it together.

WW

"Can't we just light it up with a match?" Walter asked.

"Charlie, honey, listen to me." Charlie's mother knelt down on the floor next to him. "This needs to stop. You've become obsessed. It's going to affect your schoolwork and—"

"Mom, do you really think this is the time to talk about it?" Charlie stared directly into his mother's eyes, causing her to flinch. "Right now, we've got to find some way to keep those dogs out of the room, and then Walter and I have to try to get rid of this book." He smacked his backpack. "But the one guy who could help us is in— Wait a minute." He spun back around. "Conrad, Minnesota! That's just across the Iowa border. No more than forty miles away. We could be there in, like, an hour!"

"Why do we want to go there?" Walter asked. "Even if we could burn up the book, do you think those demons will stop chasing us around? We'll just tick them off even more!"

"Wisdom Willows will know what to do. If destroying the book isn't enough, he could probably help us figure out how to send word to the Academy about everything Alton's been doing. They'll send us more protection!"

"You really think this Wisdom guy knows how to do that?"

"He's a genius. He knows everything there is to know about the paranormal world."

"Who are you talking to?" Mr. Dewdle's voice boomed above the roar of dogs, sending the birds back into a squawking frenzy. "I've had it! No more talk of spirits or demons or any weird books!" He grabbed Charlie's arms and lifted him to his feet. "We are going to climb out the window, and then we're going to call animal control. After that, you're going to the hospital!"

"But, Dad—"

"Quiet!" His dad went to the window and opened the blinds. "Great! There are at least twenty more dogs down on the road. It's that dumb veterinary clinic! The door's wide open! I'm going to put them out of business, so help me! What are you looking at?" he demanded when he noticed Charlie's pale face.

The dogs were no longer the problem. Floating right outside the window were two red-robed wraiths scraping their claws against the glass.

"We are so dead!" Walter bellowed. "We need a plan, and I don't think we can wait for Ronald to help."

"What can we do? There's no way out." Charlie stared at his backpack and then around the room, searching for any form of weapon. The desk drawer contained a stapler, a couple of mechanical pencils, and half a box of paper clips. "None of this stuff will work."

From beyond the door, the scratching and snarling ceased. The hallway fell completely silent. Charlie cringed and stared at the door.

"Oh, good, maybe they're leaving." Charlie's mom perked up as she hugged Darcy around the waist.

"Come out and play, Charlie Dewdle," a high-pitched voice spoke from out in the hall.

Bumps formed everywhere on Charlie's skin. He looked at his parents, but they hadn't heard the voice.

"I'll call off the dogs if you bring out the book," the voice said.

Charlie's mom pressed her ear against the door. "I really think they've left."

"Get away from the door, Mom!" Charlie ordered. "It's not safe."

"Walter Prairie?" the voice cackled. *"Have you nothing to say for yourself?"*

"How does it know my name?" Walter asked. "We have to get out of here! I say we open the window and take our chances against the wraiths. If they're anything like the shades, we might be able to fight them off."

Charlie backed away from the desk, holding the stapler. "I'm not going to fight anything. That will just get us killed."

"Nothing is going to kill us," said Charlie's mom.

"Don't be a wuss! It's the only option we have, and I'll help you punch."

Charlie bumped into the canary cage, and the birds flapped their wings in disapproval as their feed bowl fell to the floor. "Oh boy," he said. "I think I have a better idea." Charlie opened his hand and looked down at the Feral Whistle.

Walter sighed in frustration. "We don't have time for any other ideas. And that isn't working on the dogs."

"I'm not talking about the dogs." Charlie's head slowly turned as he stared down at the metal birdcages.

Squawked

Trutti sat cross-legged on the back of a mangy pit bull, winding the whip around his wrist. Entrancing the dogs of the Kindhearted Veterinary Clinic had been his idea. *His* idea. No one else had offered any suggestions. Hoonga had just said to keep the boy trapped until the rainstorm began. But trying to contain a human possessed by an Academy Agent was no walk in the park.

Now, with the boy boarded up in his apartment with no way to escape, Trutti had a brand-new idea. He was going to capture Charlie and *The Summoner's Handbook* and take them personally to Hoonga. His master would be pleased for sure. Maybe he would reward Trutti. Maybe he would finally throw away his awful game of Bones.

"I'm waiting!" Trutti called to the boy. "You have three minutes, and then I bring in all the dogs." This was fun. All around him, his canine army stood at attention. Trutti loved dogs. Not because they so closely resembled his own shape and image, but because of how easily he could control them. Dogs worked differently from most animals. Trying to entrance even a single cat could exhaust his energy. Horses, cattle, lizards were way too difficult to use. Other than birds, dogs were by far the easiest animals for entrancement.

The study door opened, and Trutti sat up, surprised. He assumed he would have to resort to more difficult strategies to lure the boy and the prize out of the room.

Someone tossed out a small blue object, which thudded against the floor. Then the door slammed shut.

The dogs began to pant.

"What is that?" Trutti peered over the head of the pit bull.

The tiny object stood up, shook its head while making a sound like an angry rattlesnake, and then flapped its blue-feathered wings. Twenty-four pairs of dog eyes came into focus, the red glow of entrancement instantly worn off. Their hind legs bristled, and long streamers of drool plopped from their eager mouths to the floor.

"Oh bother!" Trutti groaned as the ancient blue parakeet took flight, heading for the open apartment door with the dogs stampeding after it. Right toward Trutti.

The Wraith Festival

Four yellow canaries and two gray finches stood at attention along the desktop in front of the computer. The color of their pinprick eyes had changed from black to brilliant lavender. Charlie's parents and sister stood a safe distance away from the birds and eyed them suspiciously.

"What's wrong with them?" Darcy asked as she cowered behind her mother's arm.

Charlie stood up from checking under the doorway. "The coast seems clear. I don't see any dogs out there anymore. I think they took the bait."

"I hate to admit this, but that was pretty smart," Walter said. "How did you know the dogs would chase your dumb birds?"

Charlie smiled. "I didn't. I just assumed Doris might be able to distract them. That was totally unexpected."

"Those dogs must really hate your birds."

"I know. It's so annoying. I just hope Doris's wings don't

give out on her and she ends up some poodle's snack." He returned to the desk and stared at the remaining birds. "Step aside, please," he whispered. The birds immediately obeyed, hopping out of Charlie's way as he took hold of the keyboard.

"How . . . how . . . ?" his dad muttered. "How are you doing that?" Seeing Charlie suddenly take control of the minds of his seven pet birds stunned his parents into a reverent silence. Either it was some elaborate magic trick worthy of Las Vegas, or their son had told the truth.

"You can't see it," Charlie said as he held up the invisible whistle. "But this is a Feral Whistle. We use it to control animals."

"So what you're saying is you have been possessed by an . . . um . . . an angel?" his mother asked.

"Tell her I'm not an angel, I'm an Agent. A-gent," Walter said firmly.

"That will just confuse her," Charlie answered.

"This can't be good," Charlie's mother whimpered. "Does he make you do things you shouldn't?"

Charlie opened his mouth and then closed it. She had a point. "No, Mom, it's nothing like that. He's actually a good guy."

"But why? Why would this spirit . . ."

"Walter," Charlie said. "His name's Walter."

"Right, Walter. If he's so good, why would he *possess* you? Maybe we should call one of those hotlines. What do you think, Martin? Do you know someone who could help Charlie?"

Mr. Dewdle, not looking away from the birds, grunted and shook his head. "I don't like any of this. It's not natural."

"Charlie, buddy, I hate to break up this family moment, but how long do you think ol' blue Doris is going to hold up? We need to get moving to a safer place," Walter said. "Like, now!"

"I know, I know. I think I have a good idea of where to go." Charlie clicked on the `Chat with Wisdom` link on SpiritSpy.org and typed a brief message.

`Wisdom, we need to meet. Are you there?`

"Who's Wisdom?" Mr. Dewdle whispered to his wife. "Sounds like a creep."

"He's one of Charlie's friends, dear. I'm sure he's fine."

"But why doesn't he hang out with real people at his school?" Mr. Dewdle asked. "Why does he have to type to imaginary people on the Internet?"

"I'm in the room." Charlie covered his eyes with his hand. "I can hear you!"

A response blipped on the screen.

`Charlie!`

`All is well, I hope. I'd love to meet.`
`Are you attending the Wraith Festival?`

`Yes,` Charlie typed. `Where are you staying?`

Out of the corner of his eye, Charlie saw Darcy waving her hand in front of one of the canaries. The bird gave no response even when she poked it in the chest with her finger.

"Please don't touch them, dork," Charlie scolded.

Darcy stuck out her tongue and scowled.

"I love your family," Walter said.

```
I'm at the Ritz-Carlton in Conrad. Room
406. Here's a link for the directions.
Will you be bringing the book?
```

"Ask him about the torch," Walter said.

Charlie nodded as he typed.

```
Yep. Do you have a Chamber Torch we can
use?
```

From outside the study door, a single dog barked. Darcy checked beneath the door and giggled. "It's the cocker spaniel. Can we let him in? I think he's friendly." Charlie's parents shook their heads. "Awww!" Darcy huffed and stomped her foot.

Wisdom responded.

```
Yes, I brought one in case you got my
email in time and could come. When
should I expect you?
```

"Good question," Walter said. "Is there a bus you can take from here to Conrad, Minnesota?"

Charlie gnawed on his lip and slowly looked up at his parents. "Do you think you could drive me?"

Mrs. Dewdle knelt down next to Charlie. "If you need to go to Conrad, I could probably rearrange my schedule tomorrow. When do you need to go?"

Charlie clenched his teeth and fretted. "Um . . . now."

"Now? Like right now? Charlie, it's almost nine o'clock. Can't it wait until tomorrow?"

"No, Mom, it can't. I don't think we'll survive until tomorrow."

"Don't be so dramatic."

"I'm serious. You saw what just happened." Charlie walked to the window and opened the blinds, instantly cowering away from the sight. "And you can't see them, but right outside this window are two creatures called wraiths that want to kill us. All of us!" He closed the blinds, and the wraiths began scratching their claws once more against the glass.

"*That's* obnoxious," Walter muttered.

Charlie's mom puffed out her cheeks and tapped her lip with her index finger. "It's a festival?"

"Yes. It's called the Wraith Festival. Wisdom Willows will be there, and he'll know what to do with the book. Please, Mom, I'm begging you." Charlie clamped his hands together pleadingly.

Mrs. Dewdle looked at her husband. "What do you think?"

He didn't answer, but Charlie's sister started hopping up and down excitedly. "I want to go! I want to go! Please, Mom, please!"

"Darcy, shush!" Mrs. Dewdle snapped. She stood and placed her hand on her husband's forearm. "Dear, we should probably do as Charlie says. It sounds serious."

Mr. Dewdle blinked. "Do we have to dress up?"

Getaway

Charlie, his mother, and his sister stood on the main level of the apartment complex, staring out the back-door window. Charlie's dad sat in the driver's seat of the idling family SUV beneath the covered parking lot, drumming his fingers impatiently on the steering wheel. Above the apartment, dive-bombing the remaining dogs from the Kindhearted Veterinary Clinic, Charlie's canaries and finches darted through the air, each of them still entranced by the Feral Whistle. So far, no injuries had befallen any of his pets, but Charlie worried one of the larger dogs, a Doberman pinscher or a greyhound, was bound to catch a bird in its snapping jaws.

Mr. Dewdle honked the horn and rolled his hand in the air, signaling the family to get moving.

"Yes, dear, we're coming!" Charlie's mom said, exaggerating the words so that her husband could see her mouth. "Charlie, what are we waiting for?"

Charlie checked the sky for signs of wraiths. When they had exited the study, the creepy specters were still scraping the window with their claws. He just hoped they wouldn't figure out the plan.

"Do you think they're going to try to ambush us?" Walter whispered.

"It looks clear. I don't see them," Charlie said. "And we can't stay here."

"Are you talking to Walter right now?" Charlie's mom asked. Charlie nodded. "What's he saying?"

"He's worried the wraiths might ambush us."

She frowned. "Now, you listen to me, Walter!" Her voice boomed in Charlie's ear. "Stop scaring my son!"

"Mom, you don't have to yell!"

Walter laughed. "Your mom's a trip. Is she always this . . . odd?"

"She means well."

"What's he saying now?" his mom demanded.

"Nothing."

Charlie's dad blared the horn once more, stuck his head out the car window, and yelled, "Let's go!"

The three of them, plus Walter, reached the vehicle without incident. Charlie's mom sat in the front next to his father, and Darcy sat crammed against the far window, cautiously watching Charlie as though she feared a ghost would pop out of him at any minute. The SUV lurched onto the road, and the dogs scattered. Though they nipped and barked at one another, keeping their eyes on the sky in search of the birds, Charlie could no longer see the faint glow in the dogs' eyes.

"Where is this place again?" Charlie's dad asked. "In Conrad?"

"Yes, Dad. Wisdom's staying at the Ritz-Carlton." Charlie handed him the address. Charlie's dad shook his head, sighing, but typed the information into the car's GPS and started driving.

The two red figures floating by the apartment window suddenly turned and swooshed toward the road.

"Man, they can move!" Walter said. "They're going to catch us!"

"Faster, Dad, faster!" Charlie shouted as the wraiths flew behind the SUV, their claws outstretched, raking the bumper.

"I can't go more than thirty. This is a neighborhood." He glanced sideways at his wife. "This is ridiculous," he hissed under his breath.

"Just do it." Charlie's mom nudged her husband's arm with her hand.

Mr. Dewdle shrugged. "We're going to get pulled over. But . . ." He stepped heavily on the gas pedal, and the SUV sped forward.

Forty miles per hour. Fifty. Then sixty, and seventy. Charlie watched the needle on the speedometer rise as the gap between the rear bumper and the two determined wraiths widened. When the SUV hit eighty miles per hour, the wraiths surrendered their chase and disappeared from view.

"That's about all she'll give us," Mr. Dewdle said. "This kind of SUV isn't made to go more than eighty."

"It's okay, we lost them," Charlie said.

Charlie's mom ran her fingers through the hair at the

back of his dad's head and smiled. "You did good, sweetie. You'll have to slow down a little when we hit the junction, though. You don't want to miss the turnoff to the Chapmans'. Boy, will I hear about this at the next PTA meeting. Taking Charlie to a festival and allowing Darcy to sleep over at the last minute. It's going to take a lot of explaining to keep those women quiet."

"Mom, I don't want to go to the Chapmans'!" Darcy whined. "I want to go with you guys to the festival!"

"We'll probably need to stop for gas too." Charlie's mom ignored Darcy's pleading. "Plus, I need to use the restroom."

"You've got to be kidding me," Walter groaned.

"Mom, you're just going to have to hold it," Charlie said.

A Pleasant Surprise

Conrad, Minnesota's claim to fame was that it had the largest outdoor ice-skating rink in the continental United States. It also had not one but two goat-milking farms. Regardless of those two pages in the three-page visitor's pamphlet available at all rest stops and gas stations between Conrad and Gabbiter, the attraction on the third page was the town's most popular.

The annual Wraith Festival.

Hundreds of costume-wearing paranormal fans were flooding the quiet streets of Conrad. Decorated floats of haunted houses, tombstones, and every frightening creature imaginable were parked along the curb awaiting the next morning's parade.

"What a crock!" Charlie's dad grumbled as he negotiated the SUV through the tight space between two parade floats. "Who are all these freaks?"

Charlie kept quiet in the back. He had always dreamed of

attending the festival. But at the moment, he couldn't enjoy the sights. He and Walter needed to work out the particulars of their grand scheme.

"Okay, we're going to have to be extra careful out there," Walter said. "With everyone dressed up in cloaks and hoods, it'll be hard knowing whether or not we're about to be attacked by wraiths."

"I know," Charlie whispered. "What about my parents?"

"What about them?"

"Should they go in there with me?"

"It's not the worst idea. At least they'll know if something bad happens."

"We're coming with you, whether Walter likes it or not." Charlie's mom glared from the front seat. "It's not an option."

"Relax, Mom, he wants you guys to come."

"Oh." She wiggled her nose and half smiled.

Charlie's dad looked disgusted. "Would you stop talking about this Walter kid? Please?" He steered into a public parking lot and turned off the car.

Among the hundreds, possibly thousands of Wraith Festival attendees, the Dewdles stood out like a coffee stain on a pair of perfectly white slacks.

"Don't get too far ahead of us, Charlie!" Charlie's mom shouted above the noisy street. "And don't talk to any"—she recoiled at the sight of an eight-foot-tall, fur-covered man walking on stilts—"any, er, strangers. Oh my, what exactly are *you* supposed to be?" she asked the man. He released a guttural growl, staying true to character.

"Come on, Dana!" Mr. Dewdle urged. "This whole town's been taken over by crazies."

They arrived at the Ritz-Carlton hotel, but a crowd of people had surrounded the entrance. Masked demons and ghouls chanted and held up signs that said WISDOM FOR PRESIDENT and KING OF THE WRAITH FESTIVAL.

"How are we supposed to get in there?" Walter asked. Several police officers stood at the parking lot entrance, preventing anyone from getting through.

"I guess we could ask," Charlie suggested. He pressed through the throngs of fans. "Excuse me. Excuse me!" he asked one of the officers.

"Yeah, kid, what is it?"

"I need to get in there to see Wisdom Willows," Charlie explained.

"Right. You and the rest of these people. Look, if you're not on the list, you're not getting in."

"My name's Charlie Dewdle. I don't think I'm on the list, but I know Wisdom would want to see me."

The officer smirked. "Sure, kid. Whatever."

"Well, this was a waste of time," Charlie said to his parents. "They're only letting people in who are on some list."

"And you're not on the list?" his mom asked.

"Of course he's not on the list, Dana." His dad threw his hands up in frustration.

"Charlie, look over there," Walter said.

Charlie flinched. "Look over where?"

"To your left. Is that who I think it is?"

Charlie turned to see who Walter was talking about and his mouth fell open. The girl standing a few people over looked shockingly familiar. She was wearing a long black robe and a witch's hat, but there was no doubt it was her.

"Melissa?" he called.

Melissa turned her head, and a confused look formed on her face.

"Go over there!" Walter urged.

Charlie asked his parents to stay put, then nervously walked over to Melissa.

"Charlie? I didn't know you were here at the festival."

"We . . . uh . . . just showed up."

"It's amazing, huh? I come every year. I heard they sold more tickets this year than the past three festivals combined."

"You've got to be kidding me," Walter muttered. "She's a freak, just like you!"

"I didn't know you liked this sort of thing." Charlie couldn't believe it. Melissa Bitner was into paranormal stuff? How did he not know this? They had gone to the same school since kindergarten.

Melissa gnawed on the inside of her cheek. "Yeah, well, it's kind of a secret. Only a few people know about it."

"Oh, right. I won't tell a soul," Charlie promised.

She giggled. "Don't worry. I don't care *that* much. Some of my friends already know."

"Are they here too?" Charlie's head darted around, searching for the other popular girls.

"Are you serious? They wouldn't be caught dead in a place like this. Can you imagine Sydney Mullins wearing a costume?"

Charlie shook his head.

"Sydney Mullins? Haven't met her yet, but she sounds like the kinda girl I'd rather hang out with," Walter said.

"Hey, I'm sorry about the other day." Melissa touched

Charlie's arm. "You know, when I snapped at you for break-ing Mo's hand?"

"Oh yeah, don't worry about it," Charlie managed.

"I know he probably deserved it, but I just"—she pursed her lips—"I just can't stand bullies and violence. I hated that you stooped to his level."

"It was a one-time thing," Charlie said.

Someone exited the hotel, and the crowd erupted, but it was a false alarm.

"He's supposed to make some sort of speech," Melissa said. "At least, that's what he said on his website. Wisdom Willows, that is."

"Who else is staying in the hotel?" Charlie wondered.

"There was a dinner earlier," Melissa explained. "Really ritzy. I think the tickets were like a thousand dollars apiece just to get in. Hey, this is awesome! Now we'll have some-thing else to talk about at school other than our Spanish teachers."

Charlie felt his knees wanting to knock together. "Uh-huh."

"Hey, lover boy?" Walter spoke up. "We should probably find another way in to see Wisdom."

Charlie nodded quickly. "So, what are you doing here at the hotel?"

Melissa pointed to her cardboard sign. She had painted the words MARRY ME, WISDOM! across the front. "It's just a joke. I mean, he's old, eww, but Wisdom Willows is amaz-ing!"

"Yeah, he's a paranormal icon!" Charlie agreed.

"I know! I saw him arrive this afternoon in a black limousine. It's parked toward the rear of the hotel. If he doesn't come out this entrance soon, I'm going to see if he comes out the back way. Then my sister will take me in her car to follow him." She pointed to an older girl a little ways off. "She doesn't have a choice. I covered for her last week when she snuck out on a school night with her boyfriend to Lavender Falls. If my parents ever found out, she'd lose her cell phone and her car keys. She owes me."

"I'm actually here to see Wisdom myself."

She smiled. "You and everyone else."

"No. I have an appointment." Charlie glanced over and saw the police officer he had spoken to earlier, motioning for him to approach the gate.

"You're kidding, right?" she asked, baffled.

"Charlie Dewdle?" the officer called out above the surging crowd. "Mr. Willows will see you now."

"What?" Melissa squealed. "Oh my gosh! What's it about? How did you get an appointment with *Wisdom Willows*?"

Charlie felt his skin prickle with goose bumps. "I'll have to tell you later. Where are you going to be in an hour or so?"

"Where do you think?" She grinned mischievously.

"Right! If you're still around, I'll find you."

Wisdom Willows

"Holy moley!" Charlie's dad whistled through his teeth once they'd gotten inside the hotel. "Your friend's staying here? This place is fancy."

Thick columns beneath a decorated awning marked the entrance of the check-in office. An assortment of expensive vehicles—Mercedes-Benzes, BMWs, and Porsches—filled most of the parking stalls. One of the police officers led the Dewdles up the steps and into the illustrious hall.

"Wisdom Willows is the most famous paranormal researcher in the country," Charlie said. "Maybe even the world. He has hundreds of thousands of fans, and he's the keynote speaker at the Wraith Festival this year. All those people outside are here because of him."

"Wow!" Charlie's mom exclaimed, impressed. "And he's your friend?"

"Yeah, well, not exactly." Charlie shifted in his seat. "But finding *The Summoner's Handbook* is huge. It's like the biggest paranormal find ever. And I found it, so . . ."

"Ooh, look at me!" Walter mocked. "Aren't I the big cheese?"

Charlie felt severely underdressed. The guests of the Ritz-Carlton looked dolled up for some sort of expensive dinner. They wore suits and dresses, but each of them also wore masks as though they were attending a creepy masquerade ball.

Charlie watched his dad, still dressed in his work uniform, snag a steaming cookie from a plate at the front desk, much to the alarm of the receptionist.

"Can I help you?" she asked from behind the counter.

Charlie's dad stared at her, munched his cookie, and said, "No, I don't think so."

Thunder rumbled in the distance.

"Did you hear that?" Walter asked.

Charlie nodded. "Yep, we better hurry."

The officer escorted them to room 406, then left to return to his post. The gold trim of crown molding sparkled around the opening of the door.

"Fancy," Mr. Dewdle said breathlessly as Charlie knocked on the door.

"Just let me handle this, okay?" Charlie whispered quickly. "Don't do anything to embarrass me."

"Really?" his mom said.

The door opened, and a skinny man, maybe midforties, with short black hair parted down the middle, greeted the Dewdles. He had a thin mustache and wore brown-rimmed glasses and a fanny pack around his waist.

"Good evening!" the man said, and then a look of surprise filled his eyes when he saw Charlie's parents. "Oh my, so many of you!"

"Hello," Charlie's mom said. "Are you Charlie's friend Willie?"

The man's eyes, magnified by the thick lenses, blinked in confusion.

"Mom, his name is Wisdom." Charlie covered his eyes with his hand.

"Sorry," she whispered. "Mr. Wisdom, nice to meet you."

Wisdom Willows offered a slight bow. "Welcome to my humble lodgings. I am pleased to make your acquaintance."

"What a dork," Walter mumbled. "Is that a fanny pack? Do people still even wear those things?"

Wisdom's mustache twitched, and his eyes darted among the three Dewdles as if unsure who to greet first. Then he shook his head and held out his hand. "You must be Charlie. And are these your parents?" Charlie's dad and mom shook Wisdom's hand in turn. "Lovely! I trust you found the hotel easily enough? Come in, come in!" The group entered Wisdom's room. "What did you think of all the wonderful decorations for the festival?"

Charlie's dad smirked. "Some might call them decorations, while others would call them pieces of—"

"You loved them, didn't you, Dad?" Charlie eyed his father.

"Sure," his dad said. "I was going to say pieces of art." Then he fell silent.

"I understand you've got quite a problem," Wisdom said. "Did you bring it? Is it . . . in there?" He gestured eagerly to the backpack. Charlie nodded, and Wisdom's eyes lit up brighter. "Well, well, sit down, make yourselves at home. I should have some room service here shortly. Stuffed squash, pickled beets, venison."

"Ick!" Charlie's dad made a sour face, and his wife swatted his chest with the back of her hand.

"Sit, sit!" Wisdom said again.

Seated at a table in a kitchen almost larger than the one in the Dewdles' apartment, Charlie gazed around the room. Wisdom Willows had set up tons of electronic equipment. Computer towers and monitors, radio-transmitting devices, giant EMF detector screens with green squiggly lines bouncing and chirping. He had plastered the walls with poster-sized photographs of hazy paranormal images and ramshackle buildings. A dry-erase board with scribbled words and symbols stood next to a leather couch.

Wisdom flourished his hand behind him. "Yes, my work never ceases, even when I'm on somewhat of a . . . vacation. But never mind that. Let's look at the item. Charlie's mom, Charlie's dad, if it's all right with you, may I discuss this with Charlie alone?"

"Alone?" Charlie's mom said, and looked warily at her husband. "You want us to leave?"

"Oh no! That would be absurd. Why don't you have a seat in the living room and watch some television while we wait for our food. There's bound to be some sort of sporting event going on somewhere."

Mr. Dewdle brightened. "That should be fine. Come along, Dana. Let's see if we can catch the last of the Royals game." They wandered into the next room, and a few moments later, the television clicked on. Charlie could hear a muffled conversation begin and his father grumble something incoherent.

Wisdom's lips stretched thin. "Ah, it's the blue button on the controller. That'll change the channel," he said, which seemed to satisfy Charlie's parents.

"So, may I see it?" Wisdom stroked the end of his mustache with a ringed finger. From outside, a gentle patter of raindrops commenced against the window. The storm had reached Conrad early.

"It's raining," Walter whispered. "Keep an eye out."

Charlie unzipped the backpack and slid the heavy, ancient book across the table. Wisdom pressed the tips of his fingers together before gingerly opening the cover. Several moments passed as he perused, his smile growing wider and wider after each page. When he glanced at the page at the end containing the smaller characters, he gasped. Then he sniffed the book, his nostrils flaring wider with each breath.

"What's he going to do next? Taste it?" Walter asked.

"How rude," Wisdom muttered, looking up quickly from the book. "I didn't even offer you a drink. Would you like a soda? A juice? Some ice water?" He clinked the ice in his glass.

Charlie shook his head. "No, I'm not thirsty."

"This is indeed a treasured find." Wisdom patted the book. "Tell me again where you found it?"

"In a hole behind an abandoned shopping mall."

Wisdom laughed. "Indeed! A shopping mall? In Gabbiter, Iowa, of all places." He seemed genuinely impressed.

"Yeah, I know." Charlie still felt completely starstruck, sitting this close to such a celebrity. Wisdom Willows was discussing paranormal matters as if Charlie were one of his most trusted friends. "Mr. Willows?"

"Come now. Call me Wisdom."

"Wisdom. I think there's something else dangerous going on with this book."

"You do?"

"Yeah. We—I—think there's a conspiracy at the Afterlife Academy."

Wisdom leaned slightly forward. "How intriguing! Why do you think that?"

"Well, there's this guy named Alton. And I think he may have done something to try to get control of *The Summoner's Handbook*."

"You need to tell him more than that!" Walter chimed in. "At least tell him where Alton works."

Charlie flared his nostrils. How was he supposed to explain to Wisdom how he knew Alton without revealing anything about Walter? Would Wisdom believe Charlie if he told him he had a Guardian Agent?

"Let's discuss your theory in a moment." Wisdom drummed his fingers on the book. "Now, back to this. You said you've read some of the pages."

"Uh . . . yeah," Charlie said.

"The one in the back?" Wisdom clarified. "The decoding page?" He opened the book and pointed anxiously to the back page.

"Just like you said."

"And you can read this whole book now?"

Charlie scratched his head nervously. Hadn't he already explained all this to Wisdom online?

"Charlie, I think there's something wrong," Walter muttered. "Have you ever told Wisdom that you live in Gabbiter?" he asked. "I don't remember you writing that online."

Wisdom's head tilted slightly to the side. "I don't like your friend, Charlie," he whispered. "Please tell him to keep quiet."

Charlie opened his mouth to question, but someone knocked on the door.

"Ah, room service. It's about time. I'm sure you're famished!" Wisdom stood and left the kitchen.

"What's going on? Doesn't this seem weird to you?" Walter asked frantically. "He totally heard me!"

"Yeah, maybe, but I think he could be talking about something else. He is kind of odd. Maybe he wasn't talking about you."

"Wake up, dude! Willows can hear me!"

"I can't be the only one who can hear spirits. Maybe it's more normal than we think."

Walter scoffed. "It's not normal!" He paused. "Where's *The Summoner's Handbook*?"

Charlie's eyes shot toward the table where Wisdom had been sitting. He bent over and looked underneath each of the chairs.

"I guess he must've taken it with him to the door."

Lightning and thunder erupted outside, and rain began to pour, pelting the hotel with a deluge of water.

"Why would he do that? Why would he take the book?"

But before Charlie could answer, Wisdom pranced back into the room, clutching *The Summoner's Handbook* in his arms.

"See?" whispered Charlie.

"Who's ready for dinner?" asked their polite host.

But Charlie didn't even hear what he said. Standing behind Wisdom was a massive form that filled the room from floor to ceiling. At least nine feet tall, the creature had golden-brown skin, muscular arms, and gigantic tusks jutting from its mouth. A single bloodshot eye blinked at the top of its face as it gazed hungrily down upon Charlie.

"Charlie and, ah, Walter Prairie, I believe"—Wisdom gestured with his hand to the monster—"I'd like you to meet my friend Hoonga." He pulled a large, glowing purple orb from his fanny pack, which Charlie immediately recognized as an enormous piece of Celestial stone. "Make it quick!" Wisdom commanded.

Charlie stared. How was *Wisdom* involved in this?

"Running would be great right about now!" Walter shouted.

But Charlie couldn't move. The betrayal of his idol and the sight of the Cyclops was too much for him. His blood seemed to stop pumping through his veins, and he stood stone-still.

With a motion faster than the lightning striking, Hoonga thrust his hand through Charlie's chest and yanked Walter out of him.

41

A Visit to an Old Friend

The giant demon had Walter trapped in his hands. Powerless, he watched two other creatures with lizard heads and wiry insect arms and legs crash into the hotel room and seize Charlie, who was knocked unconscious when the demon removed Walter. He flopped around like a rag doll as one of the demons tossed him over its shoulder. From out of the living room, four more disgusting demons emerged, carrying Charlie's parents. They were bound with thick cords and appeared to be unconscious as well. Walter couldn't understand how the demons could carry them. Charlie was different from other humans because of his involvement with *The Summoner's Handbook*. But the creatures shouldn't have affected Charlie's parents, unless the demons in Wisdom's hotel had somehow become unusually powerful. Did the sudden influx of power come from Wisdom's control? Had he used the book?

Ronald hadn't exaggerated when he'd said reversing a

spiritual possession was painful. Walter's arms burned from Hoonga's touch, and he whimpered in pain. He knew Charlie had felt it as well, from his screams when Hoonga yanked them apart and the fact that he'd lost consciousness. Walter had failed.

Utterly failed.

Had it happened when he'd first arrived on the scene, Walter would've chalked it up to a rookie mistake and moved on. But now Charlie was his friend. What would happen to him? What would happen to his family?

"Take care of him," Wisdom ordered the demon he'd called Hoonga. "Then meet me later to complete the ceremony."

"With pleasure!" Hoonga licked his tusks.

Wisdom commanded that the other demons carry Charlie and his parents out of the room, then turned to Walter before exiting to leave Hoonga to do his dirty work. "You've certainly been a troublemaker, haven't you? I wish I could stay and watch this, but I'm a little preoccupied. I trust you'll understand. Oh, and nice shorts."

Walter glanced down and frowned. He had forgotten all about his clothing, and he remembered how pristine Ronald had looked in his gleaming white uniform. Where was Walter's uniform? Where were his weapons for self-defense?

"I'm going to rip out your essence, wad it up into a teeny, tiny ball, and then swallow you like a lemon drop," Hoonga said once Wisdom had left.

"What's going to happen to Charlie?" Walter asked.

"Do not speak to me!" Hoonga stomped his elephant foot on the hotel floor.

"Tell me! What are they going to do to Charlie?" Walter stared defiantly into Hoonga's solitary eyeball.

A smile cracked the demon's scowl. "His soul will be absorbed into *The Summoner's Handbook,* thus opening the Gateway for my kind to enter your world with no restrictions. No complications. No more waiting for the perfect weather conditions to manifest. We will have the ability to gnash and rip apart every last one of your kind. Pure mayhem! And the world will owe your friend Charlie for making it possible."

Walter's head drooped forward. He didn't fully understand what absorbing into *The Summoner's Handbook* required, but he could guess it wouldn't bode well for Charlie.

"Let's play, shall we?" Hoonga squeezed Walter's arms in his claws.

Closing his eyes, Walter prayed for a quick destruction. Instead, he felt the grip on his arms grow limp.

"No!" Hoonga dropped Walter to the floor. The demon howled as a purple circle of light lit up the room and enveloped Walter.

"Whoa, you're a big sucker!" a familiar voice shouted from beyond the shield. Walter sat up, gaping in amazement, as seven Afterlife Agents, all dressed in white fatigues, surrounded the demon. Standing among them, squaring off fearlessly with Hoonga, were the three Logan brothers.

Flashes of brilliant light blinded the beast as the Agents inflicted all manner of battle attacks. They threw lights shaped like spears and arrows. Tossed glowing grenades that exploded upon impact. One of the Agents lashed out with a long purple whip that crackled with electricity. Shields reformed as quickly as Hoonga could bat them away. The Logan brothers had amazing skill, as did the other Agents, who appeared much older than the boys—not that that was an indication of their length of time as Agents. But Hoonga was a giant, towering over them by more than three feet.

Shaking, Walter got to his feet as his protective shield dissipated. Ronald somersaulted across the room. He fired a dagger of purple light from his hand, and it penetrated through the monster's hip. Hoonga released a deafening roar as he broke off the end of the dagger, leaving a good chunk of the material stuck in his leg.

"Don't just stand there," Riley said, barely dodging a dangerous claw strike. "Get moving!"

"Right!" Walter hopped from one foot to the other and jabbed the air with his fists. "How can I help?" This was it! Go time. The moment to test his abilities. To dive headfirst into—

"Get out of here!" Reginald shouted. "We didn't show up to save your butt just to watch you get swallowed by this overgrown walrus!" He grunted as Hoonga connected with a closed-handed strike to his chest. Reginald slid across the floor, then slowly rose to his feet, his shoulders heaving with labored breaths.

"You want me to run? I'm not gonna leave you guys! I could— Holy wicked!" Walter shouted as a long, glowing spear formed in Ronald's hand and launched toward Hoonga. The weapon pierced Hoonga's shoulder and forced the demon into a backward tumble. "How did you do that?"

"Seriously, Walter. Go!" Ronald ordered. "We'll catch up with you after we dispatch this freak of nature."

The floor of the luxurious suite shuddered as another massive monster thundered into the room. Walter looked up and, seeing Gorge, felt a fit of nausea come over him.

"Oh, great!" he shouted. "You again?"

"Master," the horned, gorilla-like red demon spoke. "Your orders?"

Hoonga had several protruding spears of light in his shoulders, hips, and calf muscles. The giant Cyclops snarled and pointed a clawed finger in Walter's direction. "Capture that one!"

Running for his life, with the demon hot on his trail, Walter zigzagged through the hotel suite. He passed the big-screen television flashing baseball highlights, two closed doors, and a bathroom until he finally shot into the master bedroom. A massive four-poster king-sized bed, with the sheets downturned and several mints on the pillows, took up most of the room. Where could he hide?

"Come here, you!" Gorge said as he stepped into the room. A hand swung out, grazing Walter's arm, and immediately lit up his body with burning pain.

Gorge swung again, but Walter dodged out of the way, then raced full-speed toward the far wall, diving straight through it and out into the rainy night air. Though he felt no pain from the four-story drop, it nearly scared him to death . . . again.

Gorge followed, landing with far more grace than Walter had. "Stop running! Let me catch you!"

"Dream on!" The large horned demon was surprisingly nimble, but Walter had gained the advantage on the outside. Now Gorge was begging Walter to slow down, and shouting something about an old maid. Gorge started to lose ground, and at last he shrank into the distance.

Walter was free. He had to save Charlie. But where was Wisdom going to conduct his demonic ritual?

Suddenly, everywhere Walter turned, a wraith appeared from the shadows. His feet skidded to a halt. The six specters hovered around him, sealing off any escape, as the horned demon lumbered down the road. Gorge stepped through the circle, wheezing.

Walter was not free, after all.

"Master Hoonga requests your presence."

"Tell Hoonga to take a flying leap!"

Gorge blinked with uncertainty. "I don't know what that means."

"It means you're not taking me without a fight!" Walter cocked his head to the side and brought his fists up. When Gorge didn't immediately attack, Walter felt his old instincts kick in. He had been in this sort of position many times before. The swarming wraiths might as well have been jeering kids on the playground, and Gorge was nothing more than a bully. Walter made a quick assessment of his opponent. The demon had strong arms and hands. Plus, he couldn't forget about the horns. However, Gorge also had skinny legs. They looked unstable, unbalanced. Walter stared into Gorge's cruel eyes, but he also noticed a slight tremble in the demon's lower lip. Was that a hint of doubt? Gorge looked like a bully unsure of who he was fighting.

Before the demon had a chance to attack, Walter led off with a right hook to the side of Gorge's mouth. Light accentuated the punch, sending electric charges through Walter's arm. It tingled, but it didn't hurt. The blow temporarily stunned Gorge, and the circle of wraiths fluttered nervously around them.

"What are you, nuts?" Gorge bellowed. "You think you can beat me?" He lashed out with a claw, but Walter ducked and delivered two more quick jabs to the monster's stomach.

"Picked the wrong Agent to mess with, didn't you?" Walter hopped effortlessly over Gorge's claws as the creature swung at his legs. He grabbed Gorge's horns and forced his knee into the demon's chin. Gorge howled and toppled over backward in a crumpled heap. "And *stay* down!" Walter brushed his hands together. Twirling around, he squared off with the closest wraith. "You want some of this? Huh? Do you?" The wraith's hooded head darted from left to right, unsure of what to do. Walter had entered his element; a fighter unafraid of any enemy. But Gorge's laughter broke his concentration.

The monster propped himself up with one massive hand. "Not bad. But you didn't really think you'd won, did you?"

Before Walter could bring his hands up in defense, Gorge lunged, his head down like a charging bull. The demon's horns were spread wide enough that they just barely missed Walter's skin, the tips grazing his shirt on either side of his body. But the full force of Gorge's skull crashed into Walter's chest, knocking the wind completely out of him. Pinned beneath a heavy weight, with Gorge on his stomach, Walter swung out blindly. But his punches made little impact. Colored lights danced in front of his face. Could spirits lose consciousness?

Demon snot and drool dripped onto Walter's neck as

Gorge grinned in victory. "Want to know what it's like to have a demon snuff out your essence?"

The demon and the wraiths began to fade from Walter's vision, then disappeared, and the dark night sky transformed into a brightly lit room.

Still woozy and delirious, Walter sat up on the white floor, blinked, and looked around. Peering down at him from his desk was Alton.

Treachery

"Are you lost?" Alton stood, placing his pen behind his ear. "This is my office."

"What?" Walter rubbed his eyes and glanced around the room. "How did I get here?"

Just as before, a tower of folders rested on Alton's desk. Alton removed his glasses, breathed on them, and wiped them on his shirt.

"Well, this is new." He placed the glasses back on the bridge of his nose. "Normally when people die they arrive here seated in one of those chairs." He nodded to the row of seats Walter had sat in when he'd first landed in Alton's office. "Are you a bit of a clumsy fellow? Is that why you're down there?"

"Alton, it's me." Walter smoothed the wrinkles from his shirt. "Walter Prairie."

Pulling the pen from behind his ear, Alton licked the

point and readied to write on his pad. "Walter . . . Prairie? Why does that sound familiar?"

Before Walter could answer, Alton shot his hand into the tower on his desk and yanked out a folder from the middle. Once again, the tower teetered precariously but righted itself before toppling. After thumbing through the folder, peering over the lenses of his glasses as he read, Alton gave a brusque nod.

"Yes, well, Walter Prairie. Here you are. Again."

"Yes," Walter answered as he raised himself to sit up and then stand.

Alton snapped the folder closed. "But why are you here? Shouldn't you be doing your thing in the Academy?"

"You know why I'm here! This is all your fault!"

Alton squinted his eyes. "*My* fault?"

"Yeah!" Walter jabbed an accusatory finger at Alton. "You're the one behind everything. I knew it."

"I assure you I have no idea what you're talking about. If you're upset with your Academy courses or your uniform size, you'll need to bring that up with your Team Leader. Did I not tell you to join the Heavenly Choir? They don't have half as many upset enrollees as the Academy."

"Stop acting like you don't have a clue what's going on. You know I never went to the Academy!"

Alton puffed his cheeks out in confusion. "Well, where did you go? Did you get lost? Was I not clear with my instructions? It's just through one door."

"You're not going to get away with this. Charlie and his

parents are in serious danger because of you. Someone needs to help them and then lock you up forever!"

Alton stood and held his hands out to silence Walter. "Keep your voice down! Do you want to disrupt the entire hall? People are being Categorized right now, a very tedious process, as you may recall, and they don't need you screaming in the background." He moved around to the front of the desk. "Now get back to your dorm. Whatever your issue may be, it is not something with which I can assist you."

"What do you want with *The Summoner's Handbook,* anyway? Huh?"

"The what?"

"Were you trying to use demons to get back at the board for not letting you into the Academy?"

Alton's eyes widened in shock. He opened and closed his mouth like a bullfrog. "Who—who told you that?"

"Just because you had to clean toilets for years, it doesn't give you the right to ruin everyone's lives!"

"Who told you *that*?" Alton began to shout. "Are they spreading rumors about me? Making fun of me to the new cadets? Is that what they're talking about nowadays at the—at the—watercooler?"

The door to Alton's office opened with a bang, and Darwin Pollock stepped through. He was wearing the same three-piece suit with a gold watch dangling from a chain in his pocket that he was the last time Walter had seen him. He approached briskly and with purpose.

"Walter, you're here." Darwin exhaled a slow breath.

"Darwin! Thank goodness!" Walter had to explain things

as fast as he could. He had no idea what was happening to the Dewdles at that very moment.

Alton cleared his throat. "Mr. Pollock, why is Walter here?"

Darwin looked from Alton to Walter.

"I don't know why I'm here, but you do," Walter said to Darwin. "Alton's just playing stupid. It was because of his pop quiz that I graduated from the Academy in record time and got assigned to an HLT who'd found the—"

"One moment, Walter," Darwin interjected. "Alton, it seems that Walter and I have some things to discuss. And you look tired."

"Tired?" Alton nibbled a thumbnail. "I am. I'm always tired."

"Why don't you take a break?"

Pausing midchew, Alton spat a piece of nail out of the corner of his mouth. "Take a break, sir?"

"Yes, take a walk, a stroll."

"But I never take breaks. In fifty years, not once have I taken a break."

"Alton." Darwin's eyebrows rose.

"Well, I guess I've always wanted to see the nurseries. That could be fun." Alton placed his pen on the desk and started to smile. "Ooh, and the processing factory! But it could take hours to see all of that. How long do I—"

"Just go!" Darwin snapped, his usually calm demeanor cracked.

"Yes, sir." Alton made a quick check of his office space and then waved goodbye to Walter as he exited the room.

Standing alone with Darwin in the quiet office, the events of the last week replayed in Walter's mind. He had been inches away from certain destruction, and now he had come full circle. "How did I end up back here? In Alton's office?" he asked.

"I brought you here as soon as I saw what was happening down there." Darwin leaned against the desk. "What a disaster!"

"I know, I'm sorry! I tried to help Charlie out and protect the book, but I don't think I really know what I'm doing. Maybe I could've used some training, or a weapon or two. I don't think I'm a natural."

Darwin laughed. "A natural? Of course you're not a natural. There's no such thing!"

Job Security

Walter wasn't sure if he had heard Darwin correctly. "I'm not a natural? But you said—"

Darwin stomped his foot. His face had grown hard, and his eyes burned. He looked altogether different from the man Walter had first met. "And you certainly made a mess!"

"I just did what I was supposed to do."

"What you were *supposed* to do was leave things alone! What is it with you? Do you have a death wish? Any right-minded Agent would've realized he was in way over his head when he saw the Dark Omen summoning and would've sat it out until he could be rescued. But no!" He flailed his hands about in the air with disgust.

"What are you talking about? Why wouldn't you want me to do anything? Do you know that the demons are about to get possession of *The Summoner's Handbook*?"

"Of course I do. I am the head assigner of Agents for the HLTA."

Walter shook his head. "So Alton had nothing to do with it? You're the one who's behind everything? Why would you let the demons get ahold of the book? Don't you know what they'll do with it? Isn't the Afterlife Academy supposed to fight *against* the creatures from the Underworld?"

Darwin massaged the bridge of his nose. "That's a lot of questions for an insignificant, meddling, troublesome boy."

"You sent me to do a job you didn't want me to do! Why?"

"You really are stupid, aren't you? Do you think I can just allow a demonic summoning to transpire without offering protection? There are rules and procedures. Those sorts of things don't go unnoticed by the higher-ups! I had to send an Agent. So I picked one I *thought* wouldn't be any trouble."

"But weren't they going to notice that I'd barely died and had no training from the Academy?"

"Not if I fabricated your records. On paper, you graduated at the top of your class. No one would know. The plan would've worked perfectly because only Alton had any idea of your true status, and he's a bumbling idiot. He's too busy applying for positions at the Academy to have any idea what's going on outside his office." Darwin smiled, and Walter realized the man was actually *proud* of what he'd done. Walter felt sick.

"Why are you doing this?"

"Why? I'll tell you *why*." Darwin ripped a slip of pink paper out of his coat pocket and waved it in Walter's face. "Do you know what this is?"

Walter squinted. "Uh, a love letter?"

"It's termination paperwork. *My* termination paperwork.

I'm being forced into early retirement." He glanced down at the slip, and Walter saw a hint of sadness in the madman's eyes. "Three hundred years of stalwart service down the drain. I climbed the ranks at the Academy. I transformed it into one of the most prestigious organizations in the Afterlife. I did that. Me! And now do you know what's going to happen? There will be a ceremony—I'm certain to receive some sort of medal or trophy or other nonsense—and then I'll be ushered into heaven. End of story." Creasing the pink paper, Darwin returned his termination slip to his pocket. His lower lip quivered as if he were on the verge of tears.

"Am I missing something?" Walter asked. "Isn't that what you want? To go to heaven?" Wasn't that what everyone wanted?

Darwin narrowed his eyes. "I was a member of the board, and they were going to make me director. I was primed to have true power and position. And because of a few paltry mistakes and what some people call 'poor decisions' on my part over the past decade, instead of a promotion I'm getting the ax! How was I supposed to know that sweet Romanian princess would end up igniting a border war? I couldn't have known that! She didn't register on any of my reports!"

Walter had been backing slowly away from Darwin and was now flat against the wall. He was too far from the door, though, and by the time he made it over, Darwin would be able to get to him. He would just have to hope that someone in one of the other rooms would hear Darwin ranting and come in. But all the doors remained closed, and Alton was taking full advantage of his break.

"Now they'll hand over my job to some pip-squeak rookie," Darwin continued. "And I'll spend the rest of eternity strumming a harp."

Walter didn't dare ask Darwin what other questionable decisions he had made the last ten years to land him in hot water, but the most recent incident involving Charlie and a one-eyed demon couldn't be helping his case.

"But you said we were linked. You said that I was the first person to score that high on the exam since when you joined the Academy. Was that another lie?"

Darwin licked his lips. "I'm afraid so."

"You could've gotten me killed—worse than killed. Ronald told me that a demon could destroy me, that I'd hardly exist for eons, and then my spirit would have to be rebuilt."

"Ah, yes."

"I guess I'm sorry you're being forced into heaven, but this still doesn't explain what any of this has to do with *The Summoner's Handbook*."

"Isn't it obvious? Job security. Increase the amount of demon attacks on earth, and suddenly the need for a seasoned veteran at the helm of the Academy becomes a necessity. They wouldn't dare place someone with zero experience in charge of recruiting and training Agents if they realize how desperate things have become. If I can control the Underworld, I can control my destiny."

All the attacks, all the problems, the run-ins with Hoonga and the rest of the monsters, and now Charlie's capture and eventual death, all boiled down to one pathetic man's attempt to keep his job? "But how are you going to control the demons? Once they have the book, that's it. They'll be in control," Walter protested.

"Ah, this is where you'll see the workings of a true genius." Darwin grinned.

"The demons aren't *going* to use *The Summoner's Handbook*. I knew that I needed to increase demon activity without things getting out of hand. The problem was that I couldn't possibly control *The Summoner's Handbook* myself. Too much contact with the book would destroy my aura. I needed a human being who would control it for me."

"But the one-eyed demon—Hoonga—he said they were going to kill Charlie. That in order to open the Gateway for the demons, Charlie's soul had to be absorbed into the book."

The intensity in Darwin's eyes softened. "Ah, a sad situation, I agree, but a necessary sacrifice."

"I thought you were kind and good—that you would be a mentor to me! But you're twisted and evil!" Walter yelled at the top of his lungs. He lunged at Darwin, but a bolt of electricity zapped Walter's body. The energy forced him to his knees, and his hands shook out of control.

"Don't! *Ever!* Touch! Me!" Darwin boomed.

"You're crazy. Your plan is crazy!"

"It's not crazy, thank you very much. It's brilliant. And Arnold is well versed in these matters and will take every precaution. He'll perform the ceremony and gain control of the demons. And I will be in control of him and have a long and happy career."

"Who's Arnold?"

"Arnold Featherstone, of course."

"*Who* is Arnold Featherstone?"

"Oh, right. Arnold is known under a different name by his faithful followers. I believe you know him as Wisdom Willows."

So *that* was how Wisdom was involved.

"You won't get away with this," Walter hissed. It was the only thing he could think to say.

"Actually, I believe I will. Just as soon as I can figure out what I'm going to do with you."

Just then, the door opened, and they heard a familiar voice.

"I am *not* a bumbling idiot, and I never take breaks!"

Darwin and Walter turned around. Standing in the doorway was Alton. And by his side, weary and bruised from battle, were Ronald, Riley, and Reginald Logan.

44

How's That for Ambition?

"Alton, don't be foolish." Darwin's fingers trembled at his sides as he squared his shoulders and stared down the office worker and three young Agents. "This won't turn out the way you hope. I assure you."

"I can't believe you're behind all this," Ronald said. He looked at Darwin for an explanation. "Why?"

"Oh, shut up!" Darwin grabbed Walter and held him in front of him. "As long as I have Walter as my hostage, I have a— Oof!" Walter had elbowed him sharply in the stomach, and he buckled over.

Breaking free from Darwin's grasp, Walter barely had enough time to move out of the way before Alton plowed headfirst into the Head Assigner of Agents. The two old men scrambled on the floor. Darwin tried desperately to get free, but Alton pinned Darwin's arms to the floor with his knees.

"How's that for ambition?" Alton demanded confidently, though he was shaking like a leaf.

A squadron of Agents escorted Darwin away with glowing manacles latched to his wrists. "Internal Affairs is going to have a field day with this!" Alton grumbled. "Which will ultimately mean more paperwork for me. Ho-hum."

"Walter, are you okay?" one of the senior-ranking officials asked.

"I think so."

"Darwin managed to successfully throw everyone off his tracks for almost a week," said the same Agent. "Until your reappearance in Alton's office, no one here knew about the resurfacing of *The Summoner's Handbook* or Wisdom's involvement. Luckily, Alton put two and two together very quickly, and the Agent Ronald Logan explained the rest. Now that we know what's been going on and how the most lethal book on earth has fallen into the possession of the demons, we are elevating Charlie's case to a class five—the highest priority."

"What's going to happen?" Walter asked Ronald. The other Logan brothers stood with the Agents.

"We've located Charlie and his parents. They're being held by Wisdom in the football locker room of Conrad High School," Ronald said.

"Are you going with them?"

"Yeah." Riley rubbed his hands together. "It's going to be a full-scale ambush!"

"I'm coming too," Walter said.

Reginald shook his head. "Sorry, man. We can't let you do that."

"You can't stop me!"

"Walter!" Riley grabbed his arm. "You're not an Agent. You haven't even completed one day of the training course."

"So? I've done more this past week than any of you have done in four years. There's no way I'm going to sit this out. Charlie is *my* assignment!"

"It's against regulations," Reginald reasoned. "You'll just get in the way."

"No, he's right," Ronald said. "Walter has done more than all three of us combined. How he survived a week protecting *The Summoner's Handbook* is nothing short of a miracle. And technically, Charlie is still his HLT. If anyone deserves to be down there, it's Walter."

Walter nodded. "Thanks, man."

"There's just one problem," Ronald continued. "There's no way we can let you go down there looking like that."

Destiny

Charlie sat chained to a metal folding chair in the middle of the Conrad High School boys' locker room. Locker doors with jersey numbers taped above them lined the walls. Everything stank of sweaty socks and underwear. Up a flight of stairs and out on the field, the decorations for the Wraith Festival's crowning celebration, the Demon Dance, were in their final preparations. Dozens of people were bustling around the stadium, draping streamers over the bleachers or tying balloons to the goalposts, without any clue as to what was taking place below.

Wisdom had tied up Charlie's parents in the shower room. Charlie couldn't see them, but he knew they were there, because they hadn't stopped arguing with each other since the three of them awoke to their current predicament.

"All this is your fault, Martin!" His mother's voice echoed in the tiled room.

"My fault?" his dad asked. "*My* fault? How is any of this my fault?"

"If you had taken more paid leave to spend a weekend with your son every now and then, none of this would've happened."

Mr. Dewdle laughed derisively. "That has nothing to do with this. If anything, it's your fault. Charlie takes after you. Always reading—"

"Oh, reading books is the culprit? Is that what you're saying?"

Charlie's chin dropped to his chest as the arguing continued. "Oh brother," he whispered.

Standing at attention by the locker room entrance, a pair of demons with alligator snouts and multiple pairs of wiry arms shook their heads in disapproval but kept quiet.

"You think *this* is bad? You should hear them at Christmas dinner," Charlie muttered.

Charlie could still see the demons despite the absence of Walter. He figured his reading of *The Summoner's Handbook* had brought on the permanent change. His parents, however, had not received the gift of sight. The two demons standing guard over them had entered the shower room several times, and his parents had continued arguing without skipping a beat.

When Wisdom Willows descended the steps and entered the room, he wore a hooded green robe and carried *The Summoner's Handbook* in his hands.

"Hello, Charlie. Good to see you. I trust you've been taken care of since arriving?"

"I've been tied up in a disgusting locker room," Charlie said. He glared at Wisdom.

"It *is* disgusting, isn't it?" Wisdom glanced disdainfully at the rows of lockers. "But this is where it all happened. The beginning, if you will, of my long, painful, but soon-to-be-glorious journey to greatness."

"In a locker room?" Charlie asked.

Wisdom sighed. "Yes. In this very locker room. With Gopher Phillips, captain of the varsity football team. I was fourteen at the time. I won't bore you with the details, but it involved what we used to call a wedgie and my underwear."

"We still call them wedgies. I get them all the time," Charlie replied.

Wisdom made a fretful expression as he knelt and placed his hand on Charlie's knee. "Bullies. What good are they? At any rate, my wedgie was inconsequential to this story. I did, however, see my first demon that awkward afternoon."

"You did?"

Wisdom nodded. "And Gopher Phillips saw it too. He denied it, of course, as the feebleminded typically do when faced with a decision that could ultimately destroy their popularity. But I knew that he saw. Once you've seen something like that, you can't hide the truth. You understand, don't you, Charlie? You've seen things now, haven't you?"

"I'm tied up in a room surrounded by demons," Charlie answered dryly.

"Yes, well, I meant you understood what it was like the first time you saw one. A creature. Unexplained. Unnatural. Yet real all the same. Do you remember the change that came over you?"

Charlie didn't respond. Wisdom's question had transported him back to that evening when he first witnessed the banshee hovering above his bed. It had terrified him, yes, but he couldn't deny the fact that something had changed inside him, in a wonderful way.

Wisdom smiled knowingly. "It was an awakening for you, wasn't it? Me too, Charlie. Finally, after years of believing in another world, I had been given a moment of proof. To this day, I have no idea why the demon appeared within these walls, but I'd like to think it was a sign, a symbol of my grand calling in life."

"What happened to Gopher?" Charlie asked.

"Gopher?" Wisdom's eyes refocused. "Why do people always ask that whenever I tell this story? Does it really matter what happened to Gopher Phillips? I'll answer that for you. It doesn't. What matters is that I triumphed. I used that demon sighting to succeed in life. And this locker room has become something of a museum for me. I think it fitting to write the next chapter of my story here, in Conrad."

Charlie nibbled on the tip of his tongue. "That's great. But why am I here?"

"My boy, you are here because of destiny!"

Charlie smirked. To think he'd once considered Wisdom a genius. An idol. Even a superhero. Not anymore. "How long have you been working for them?" He nodded at the alligator demons.

Wisdom chuckled. "I don't work for them. They work for me."

"I don't understand."

"No time to explain, Charlie. We need to begin." Wisdom

opened the book and riffled through to a dog-eared page. Once satisfied, he placed the book in Charlie's lap and pointed to one of the center paragraphs. "Now, if you will please read from here"—he dragged his finger down the page—"to here."

Charlie nudged the book off his knees. "I'm not reading anything."

Alarm altered Wisdom's features. "How dare you!" Scooping up the book, he gently dusted off the cover. "This is not some meaningless textbook that you can kick at your leisure! This is a priceless treasure, and you will treat it with respect."

"Well, then don't touch me with it, or I'll do it again!"

"Tell him to keep his slimy hands off you!" Charlie's dad shouted from the next room.

"Yes, and tell him we're going to report him to the police!" Charlie's mom chimed in. "And then we're going to file a complaint with the Conrad school board. These showers are filthy, and the mold alone could kill you!"

"Noral! Pidge! Shut them up!" Wisdom commanded. Charlie watched in horror as the two guard demons raced into the next room and silenced his parents completely.

"What are they doing to my parents?" Charlie demanded.

"Nothing. Yet. But if you don't start cooperating, I'll have Noral and Pidge pull their lips off! Read this. And don't knock it to the floor!" Wisdom placed the book once again on Charlie's knees, and Charlie had to fight the urge to spit on its pages.

46

Decked in White

W alter couldn't stop gawking at his fancy new threads. Like the other Agents, he wore stark white fatigues and a utility belt complete with standard Afterlife Academy Agent gear. Secured in one of the compartments was his very own piece of Celestial stone.

Crouching just outside the football stadium entrances, Walter, the Logan brothers, and thirty other highly trained Agents, pulled from their other assignments all over the world, planned their attack.

Despite the late hour, the stadium buzzed with excitement. Under the steady sheet of pouring rain, several demons and wraiths patrolled the area while uniformed festival workers wearing raincoats constructed a stage on the fifty-yard line, oblivious to the deadly creatures all around them.

Walter and the Logan brothers hung back while the high-level Agents took out the enemy guarding the stadium perimeter, furtively prowling up to their targets and disposing of them like skilled assassins. The dark creatures never had any inkling they were being stalked until the silenced weapons of the Agents winked them out of existence.

This continued until every watchdog demon and wraith vanished from the stadium.

"That was easy," Walter said.

"Too easy." Ronald surveyed the stadium through a pair of binoculars. "These guys were nothing. Low-level classifications."

"Willows has no idea Darwin's scheme has been discovered," said a tall, muscular, older Agent named Teague. "As it stands, we should have the element of surprise to our advantage. But that won't last long. We're picking up heavy readings of Underworld essence at the south entrance of the locker room. Wisdom must have an entire horde of demons down there. We're going to have our hands full."

"That one-eyed freak will be there, for sure," Reginald said, staring down at the painful bruises on his arms. "During our battle, I was able to tag him with a homing device. There were seven of us back at the hotel, and we hit him with everything we could, but he still got away."

The others whispered Hoonga's name with recognition and smiled as they remembered their own encounters with the giant Cyclops over the years.

"That monster's nasty!" Walter said. "Is he like the biggest and baddest of them all?"

Teague shrugged. "No. Not by a long shot, but he's one of the craftiest demon-outpost Controllers in the country. We've had that guy on our radar for over two decades."

"Then how is this Wisdom Willows lowlife controlling Hoonga?" Riley asked. "His powers are far superior."

"It's because he has a huge piece of Celestial stone!" Walter said. "It's bigger than all of ours combined."

Reginald narrowed his eyes. "No way! Where would he get a stone that big?"

"From the vault," Teague explained. "They're off-limits to the general Afterlife population, but members of the board have access."

Walter nodded. "Yeah, and Darwin's on the board."

"*Was* on the board," Teague clarified. "If Wisdom knows how to operate the stone, we won't stand a chance against him. Our only hope is to somehow get ahold of it and cause it to self-destruct."

Squatting, Teague pulled a small electronic device from his belt, and a holographic layout of the locker room appeared in the air. "The locker room has only one other exit, here." He pointed to a spot on the holograph. "It's a bottleneck. If we charge in there with our guns blazing, Wisdom will barricade the way with as many demons as possible and escape out the rear exit. If he bolts before we can tag him, we lose."

"We could come down through the ceiling," an Agent named Monroe suggested. "Create a hexagonal point of attack with strikers here and here."

"That would require subterranean travel," said the Team Leader, dismissing the idea. "How good are you guys at submersion?" he asked Walter and the Logan brothers.

Walter smiled. "Submersion? Like a submarine?"

Teague shook his head. "They're not trained for that sort of maneuver."

"We can pass through walls, if that's what you mean," Ronald said.

"Submersion is different from walking through solid objects. It requires a great deal of balance and focus. Without the proper post-Academy training, you'll be too dizzy to offer us any help against a demon horde."

"We should split up and cover both entrances," Monroe said.

Teague nodded. "Agreed. Take half of our forces here"—he pointed to a spot on the holograph—"and wait for my command. Do not get spotted. I'll take the four rookies in my squad."

"We're not rookies," Riley said. "Well, Walter is, but we know what we're doing."

"Hey, we still don't know what to do about Wisdom's massive Celestial stone," Ronald put in.

The sound of giggling arose behind them. Teague spun around in time to see two girls, one of whom was dressed in a Wraith Festival costume, approaching the locker room.

Walter's natural instinct took over as he sprawled out on the ground, trying to hide. The other Agents remained where they were. They were all invisible to the girls.

"He went in there?" one of the girls, the older one, asked.

"Yes. I just saw him! And that was his limo parked over in the lot. It's Wisdom, I promise! He must be performing a ceremony, because he was wearing robes."

"You're seriously going to go into that locker room? You're out of your mind. If Mom knew what you were doing—"

The younger girl pursed her lips. "But she's not going to find out, is she? Do I need to remind you about Lavender Falls?"

"Fine. Just don't take forever. I can't stand this place. It's like the worst Halloween party ever."

"What the heck is *she* doing here?" Walter looked on in shock.

"You know them?" Ronald asked.

"That's Melissa Bitner. She goes to Charlie's school. It sounds like that's her older sister. She must've followed the limo from the hotel."

"Well, she's about to add to our problem."

Melissa broke away from her sister and approached the stairs leading down below the stadium.

"We have to stop them!" Walter stood. He reached for his belt to search for one of his devices.

"They're mortals, Walter. They've not been exposed to the Underworld or the Afterlife. We have no means of controlling them," Teague explained.

Melissa, still giggling with excitement, crept down the stairs and opened the locker room door.

A Gathering of Demons

Charlie was trying to stall. "I thought you were one of the good guys. Your website—your books—they're about fighting the dark side. Is that all fake?" Charlie was practically foaming at the mouth.

Wisdom flinched. "Fake? I'm not a fake. I have been fighting, and I continue to do so. But do people care? I've been made fun of for years. Mocked. Ridiculed. Slandered. All because of my beliefs. Do you read the newspaper much?"

Charlie shook his head. What kid his age had time to do that?

Wisdom reached below Charlie's chair and held up a copy of the most recent newspaper. On the front page was a picture of Wisdom beaming at the camera. The headline read: WISDOM WILLOWS TO SPEAK AT ANNUAL FESTIVAL.

"That's nice."

"Hardly. Listen to this!" Wisdom spat. "'Year after year

hordes of faithful followers suit up in their creepiest costumes and arrive in Conrad to celebrate the annual Wraith Festival. What should be considered a thrilling weekend for children, however, has transformed into a broiling hive for adult weirdoes. Taking the helm at this year's nerdfest is none other than Conrad's own Wisdom Willows, the self-proclaimed king of the dimwits.'" Wisdom crumpled the edges of the paper with his hands. "And look who wrote it." He jabbed his index finger at the italicized name beneath the headline.

"Gopher Phillips?" Charlie whispered. "He works at the newspaper?"

"He's supposed to report the news. The facts. Not sway people's minds with his opinions!" Tight-lipped and red-faced, Wisdom wadded the paper into a ball.

"Who cares what he writes?" Charlie reasoned. "You're way more successful than he is. I bet most people don't even read what he writes."

"Oh, they read. They all do. And they all talk about me and about my loser minions. That includes you, Charlie. But now, after tonight, they'll know the truth. They'll see their mistakes and beg for my forgiveness."

"That's what this is all about? Because people make fun of you? Join the club. I've been made fun of my whole life. That doesn't mean it's okay to take revenge. What you're going to do will hurt people, and not just the people like Gopher Phillips." Charlie suddenly realized that Melissa Bitner had been right to be angry with him when he'd broken Mo's hand. If Charlie lived his whole life looking for the right moments to take revenge on enemies like Mo, or Vincent, or even Wheeler, he would end up being no better than Wisdom.

"Why were you trying to help me online? What was all that garbage about a Chamber Torch?" Charlie continued.

"My boy, I don't even think a Chamber Torch exists. I'm sorry I misled you, but I needed the book—and you."

"How did you even know what to do with *The Summoner's Handbook*?"

"I'm not working alone. I have a benefactor. Someone has been providing me with the necessary materials." Wisdom reached into his fanny pack and pulled out the large glowing orb. "It's the largest Celestial stone ever given to anyone, living or dead. This provides me with control over all Underworld creatures. It's not a fun place, the Underworld. It's messy."

"You've been there? Where the demons come from?"

"How else would I have been able to amass my army?"

"But I thought only monsters could travel there."

"Of course not. Anyone who knows the way can visit the Underworld. And naturally, me being me, I knew the way. But no human would ever dare step into their realm unprotected. That would be like delivering a pizza to a college fraternity, if you know what I mean." Wisdom stuck out his tongue. "But I have my stone for protection."

Wisdom tilted his head to one side. "Charlie, you and I are a lot alike."

"We are *nothing* alike!" Charlie snapped. "I'm not destroying the world with demons just because I was bullied."

Wisdom's face twisted with grief. "You don't get it. That's

not what I'm doing. I'm just opening a pipeline. Letting a little more in. Giving a select few demons extra powers to mix things up a bit. I'll keep control over them with the handbook."

"How are you going to control them when you can't read it?"

"Don't be silly. I've examined the decoding page. I can read it just fine. But only *you* can provide the soul sacrifice to open the Gateway. Once that's done, I'll have no trouble controlling the book. Then, as payment, I'll be allowed to rule the demons as I choose. Show them off to all the non-believers. My benefactor has promised to overlook it when I become one of the most powerful men on earth. I'll live a long, full life, and then I get a one-way ticket to heaven. Guaranteed!"

"Hello?" a female's voice sounded from the stairwell.

Both Charlie and Wisdom turned to focus their attention on the girl standing in the locker room doorway.

"Oh no," Charlie whimpered. Where had she come from? Melissa Bitner had picked the worst time to become interested in Charlie's life.

"Hello there, little girl." Wisdom tried to smile, but he came across looking gassy.

"You're Wisdom Willows," Melissa said, no longer looking as eager and excited as she had outside the hotel.

"That's right. Are you a fan?"

"What are you doing to Charlie?" She took another step, stopped, and stared at the bindings on Charlie's arms and legs.

"Ah, you're his sister? His girlfriend?" Wisdom asked.

"No!" Charlie's voice cracked. "She's neither one of those things."

"How long have you been hiding up there?" Wisdom pointed at the stairs with his chin.

"Long enough to hear that you're about to do something terrible to Charlie."

"Yes, well, what you see before you is just an act," Wisdom explained. "Charlie and I are practicing for our performance at the festival."

Charlie began to deny it, but Wisdom promptly slapped him on the back of the head.

"Ouch!"

"Sorry," Wisdom apologized. "I'm still in character."

"What's really going on here?" Melissa asked. "Charlie, are you okay?"

Wisdom fixed Charlie with a dangerous glare. "Think about your parents," he muttered through tight lips.

"I'm . . . I'm fine. We're just practicing, like he said." Charlie forced a smile. He wanted to rub his throbbing head.

Melissa narrowed her eyes and glanced around the room. "You're sure?"

"Yes, yes, of course!" Wisdom barked. "Now, if you don't mind, we need to practice, practice, practice."

"I don't think so." She backed toward the stairs. Charlie could see she was shaking.

"Tell me, girl, did you come here with family? Your parents?" Wisdom asked.

Melissa nodded. "Yes, my parents are outside right now."

Wisdom gazed up the stairs, his smile widening. "I don't

think so. I think you're telling a fib." He snapped his fingers. "Noral!"

One of the alligator demons bounded out from the showers. He charged right at Melissa, but since she couldn't see it coming for her, she didn't move. Suddenly she gave a yelp as Noral's clawed hand clamped down over her mouth and the demon hoisted her into the air.

"Leave her alone!" Charlie yelled. "Let her go!"

"She's seen too much." Wisdom sighed. "Put her with his parents."

Noral toted Melissa, struggling and kicking to break free, into the shower room.

"Now, Charlie, no more talkie." Wisdom pressed his fingers together. "If you value the lives of your parents and your girlfriend, you'll start reading immediately."

"She's not my girlfriend! And you're just going to hurt them anyway!"

"Cross my heart and hope to die, if you do your part, I promise not to lay a finger on any of them." Wisdom held up his hand, solemnly swearing. "Now, time for your willing sacrifice so that we may open the Gateway and transfer your soul inside."

Charlie looked at the opened pages.

"Wait, willing? I'm not willing. Not willing at all!"

Wisdom scrunched up his nose. "Eh. Close enough."

The room crowded with more demons tromping through the rear exit. A couple of globby orange demons resembling slithering Jell-O molds were the first to enter, followed by many others in a variety of shapes and sizes. Among them walked the small bat-eared demon, the horned gorilla, and the Cyclops, displaying several gruesome injuries. The Cyclops limped up to Wisdom, wincing with every step.

Wisdom threw his hands up in the air. "Hoonga, Gorge. Don't tell me Walter got away."

Hoonga snarled. "I'm not exactly in the mood to talk about it." His eye narrowed, and he reached a claw for Charlie's throat. "Why is he still breathing?"

Wisdom held up the Celestial stone, and the demons in the room shielded their eyes, cowering at its power. "Need I remind you who's in charge here? Not you! Me! So get back, and give me space! Sorry, Charlie." Wisdom paused. "That sounds funny. Sorry, Charlie." He laughed some more. "Anyway. I apologize for the distraction. Now, where were we?"

Charlie's eyes darted around the room, landing on the various creatures glaring at him. They purred and drooled. Some of them bared their teeth while others released flatulence. It was a disgusting crew of demons.

"Are we still under sufficient guard?" Wisdom asked, hiding the stone.

Hoonga shrugged. "Not really. I've pulled in my best and left a half dozen of the lesser demons and wraiths outside to watch. We'd better hurry."

Wisdom clapped his hands together. "Okay, my friend, no more delays." He once again pointed to the desired passages. "It's time to begin."

Decoy

"Any more of your friends going to show up to complicate things?" Riley asked.

Walter shrugged. "Who knows?"

Melissa's older sister sat on one of the bleachers, gabbing away to someone on her cell phone.

"We need to act before she wonders where her sister is and goes down to find her," Reginald said.

"Okay, let's split up as planned. We'll have to figure out a way to get our hands on Wisdom's Celestial stone once we're inside."

"Wait." Ronald cleared his throat. "What if we used a decoy?"

"Meaning?" Teague said.

"Well, Wisdom and the demons aren't expecting us to show up for a fight because we're not supposed to know about any of this. But they might not be too surprised to see

Walter charging in there to save Charlie. He was his HLT, after all."

Teague folded his arms. "I'm listening."

"It would be dangerous, but if Hoonga's really down there, he might want to torture Walter first for fun. It could be just the distraction we need to strike. We could dim Walter's aura with dimming powder to throw Wisdom off."

All eyes rested on Walter.

Go in alone? Allow Hoonga to capture him for torture? It sounded like a suicide mission. But if it could give Charlie a chance to make it out alive . . .

"I'm in."

"We'll have to hope that the distraction will cause Willows to drop the stone so that we can destroy it," said Teague.

"Actually, I think I have an idea about that," Walter added. "And this one's even crazier than Ronald's."

The Gateway Spell

"Why isn't this working?" Wisdom mumbled as Charlie finished reading the passage.

At that moment, an immense, hairy demon dropped through the ceiling and squished a cluster of smaller demons. Looking bewildered, the new creature stood up, knocked Hoonga over, and stomped on Trutti.

"Trutti, wake up!" Hoonga smacked the bat-eared demon's cheeks until the creature revived, blinking and dizzy.

"What happened?" Trutti whimpered with a drunken voice.

"Yes, what *did* happen?" Wisdom pored over the pages Charlie had been assigned to read. "That wasn't the Gateway spell. What did you read?"

"What you told me to read!" Charlie fired back.

Wisdom's lips moved as he read silently and his eyes darted down the page. "Oh." A look of slight embarrassment formed on his face. "Yep. Wrong one. Give me a second."

The demons murmured disgruntledly.

"Settle down!" Wisdom flashed the Celestial stone again, and the demons shielded their eyes. Charlie could tell from their angered expressions that the creatures wanted to crush Wisdom as much as they did Charlie.

"Here we are." Wisdom nodded with self-assurance. He jabbed a new page and passage with his index finger and smiled. "You can see why I'd make the mistake. They're almost identical in verbiage." He laughed, and Charlie mimicked him. The smile slipped from Wisdom's face, and he shoved Charlie's head down until his nose pressed against the page.

"Don't get cute!" he hissed. "Just read!"

Charlie stared at the words. Something felt different about this passage. He knew it in his bones. Reading those words would open the Gateway. Would change the fate of the world. Hesitating, he looked pleadingly up at Wisdom. How could he offer himself up as a sacrifice and possibly become the catalyst for global terror? He was twelve years old! He hadn't fully grown up yet. He still needed braces. Why did he have to find that stupid book in that stupid hole at Victory Junction?

Wisdom snapped his fingers impatiently, and Noral and Pidge carried Charlie's parents and Melissa into the room. Their mouths were covered, and they looked both confused and terrified.

"Don't make me do something I don't want to, Charlie." Wisdom's words flowed smooth with poison.

Charlie stared at his mom and dad. They struggled

against the firm grip of their captors, voices muffled. As much as he hated the idea of dying, watching his parents suffer would be far worse, and he'd still have to give his soul to the book.

Charlie looked at Melissa. "I'm sorry." It was all he could think to say.

Melissa was handling herself much better than the Dewdles, although even years of scouring SpiritSpy.org couldn't have prepared her for this.

Taking a deep breath, Charlie began to read. The stirring in the room ceased. Every demon held its tongue, and Wisdom's eyes twinkled with delight. The room grew intensely cold, and Charlie's breath crystallized in the air. He shivered but continued reading.

"Don't stop!" Wisdom shouted as a strong wind began to blow through the locker room. The lights dimmed as the temperature continued to drop. Charlie could sense something forming above him, a massive opening, a dark, cavernous hole, but he didn't dare look up from the pages of *The Summoner's Handbook*. He finished the first paragraph and clenched his jaw, trying not to throw up. Only a few sentences remained before the ceremony was complete. Couldn't he at least say goodbye to his parents?

Wisdom pressed a hand on Charlie's shoulder. "Almost there!"

As Charlie read, his mind pulled away from the moment. He recalled that first night when the shades had swarmed his bedroom. At that moment, his life, and the hundreds of hours he had spent investigating the world of the unexplained, the supernatural, had been validated. He had proof of something more—something outside of human beings and his normal, everyday life.

Charlie smiled as he replayed his first conversations with Walter. He couldn't believe it, but he missed that kid. If only Walter were there, Charlie knew they'd find a way out of this mess together.

"Uh, excuse me?" a voice called out.

Charlie stopped reading and looked up.

Walter Prairie was standing in the doorway.

At least thirty pairs of eyes flashed across the room.

"Have any of you seen a young boy, medium height, orange hair, freckles?" Walter continued. "A total dork."

No one moved.

"What the heck are you doing here?" Charlie asked.

"I followed you. I couldn't let you mess up the world without me at least kicking a few butts!"

Wisdom stamped his feet up and down. "Don't just stand there like a bunch of idiots!" he shouted at the demons. "Grab him!"

All at once, the demons wailed and charged Walter. Hoonga reached him first, snatching him in his arms and roaring into his face. "Foolish move!"

"Yikes!" Walter said. "You need some mouthwash."

Hoonga squeezed, and Walter gasped from the pressure. "Feel that? That's the pain of me crushing your soul. You will not survive this, boy! You will never come back from where I send you!"

Walter's lips moved, but no words escaped his mouth.

"No!" Charlie shouted.

"Don't stop reading!" Wisdom ordered. "Finish it!"

Charlie's eyes flashed from Wisdom to the book and then to Walter. "Let him go!" he demanded. "Let him go, or I'll close the book!" He nudged the book with his knees, and it threatened to fall.

"No!" Wisdom screamed. "Read it, or your parents die!"

"Let him go! Stop hurting him!" Charlie shouted.

Wisdom whirled and kicked a small scaly demon with his foot, sending it crashing into the lockers with a deafening bang.

"Argh! Let him go, Hoonga!" Wisdom commanded.

Hoonga continued to crush Walter with his arms.

"Pain!" he snarled. "Feel it draining you of life. Feel it burning in your veins!"

"Did you hear me?" Wisdom shouted. "I said let him go!"

Hoonga still refused to acknowledge the order. Wisdom stomped across the room and shoved his Celestial stone directly in front of the demon's eye. Walter fell from Hoonga's arms and scampered across the floor, gasping for breath. Wisdom kept the stone next to Hoonga for several seconds, ignoring his pleas for mercy, then pulled it away, leaving Hoonga whimpering in the corner. "You do as you're told! That's my last warning!" He brandished the stone in the faces of the other demons. "All of you! Do you hear me? Is that clear? I will have order and control. Do not force me to make an example of one of you, because I will!"

With Wisdom's attention drawn toward scolding his minions, Walter crawled over to Charlie and started untying him. "What's up?" Walter asked.

Charlie kept his eyes on Wisdom, who was parading

around with the brilliant orb pulsating in his hand. At any moment, order would be restored in the locker room, and when that happened, both he and Walter were as good as dead.

"Oh, not much."

"So you can see me now, huh?"

"Uh, yeah." Why was Walter making small talk? "Look, you shouldn't have come down here. They're going to kill all of us. Do you know you're glowing, by the way?"

"Really?" Walter stared down at his uniform. "Cool. I'm not supposed to. Teague sprayed me with some gunk to dim my aura."

"That doesn't make any sense," Charlie whispered. "And who's Teague?"

"You'll see in about twelve seconds."

"See what?"

"I still have a few tricks up my sleeve." Climbing to his feet, Walter cupped his hands around his mouth and yelled, *"Now!"*

As Wisdom stood, scolding his Underworld servants, thirty-three Afterlife Academy Agents stormed the locker room from both entrances, charging the demons and zapping them with light.

The demons crashed into one another, roaring and squealing. They clawed strips of paint from the walls and smacked lockers and benches. The tight quarters of the locker room made it almost impossible for them to dodge the Agents' weapons.

"Holy cow! Are they with *you*?" Charlie's arms now free,

he shoved *The Summoner's Handbook* off his knees, and the gaping hole in the ceiling vanished with a swirling pop.

Wisdom screamed in agony, but with all the demons and Agents scrambling around him, he couldn't make his way to collect the book. The Logan brothers circled one of the Jell-O demons and exploded it with bursts of light, spraying orange goo all over the room.

The other demons scattered. Some of them charged through the entryway, but they crashed backward into the room when they bounced into a pulsating shield the Agents had created. Noral and Pidge abandoned their post, dropping Mr. and Mrs. Dewdle and Melissa to the floor with a thud, and scampered away. The Dewdles rolled around, trying to free themselves from their bindings.

Charlie's mom's gag loosened. "The magic show has to end sometime!" she snapped. "This is not polite. You let my son go right now, Mr. Willows!"

The three of them still couldn't see any of the monsters or Agents, but they could see Charlie, who was now completely free of his bindings, and Wisdom flinching and shouting.

"Duck!" Charlie screamed. Walter dropped down just as a slime-covered snake demon, no bigger than a common raccoon, was hurled through the air by one of the Agents and skimmed across the top of Charlie's head. The demon left a trail of goop in its wake, and Charlie's hair stood on end as if doused in styling mousse.

Hoonga, already injured from his earlier fight with Walter and Wisdom's Celestial stone, took one look at the much stronger Agents, grabbed Trutti by the ears, and plowed through the middle of the chaos. Agents scattered away from his massive frame, and a sound of shattering glass rang out from the stairwell. The demon had created a gaping Hoonga-shaped hole in the shield.

Gorge fought his way out of a corner and collapsed upon Ronald, gnashing his teeth near the boy's throat. Walter reacted instinctively, and a long purple spear appeared in his hand. Charlie's mouth fell open in shock, but Walter didn't pause to admire his own creation. With an ear-piercing battle cry, he heaved the spear straight through Gorge's chest. The demon dissolved into nothing.

"Nice!" Charlie cheered.

"I know!" Walter nodded enthusiastically.

"Do you think we could untie my parents and Melissa?" Charlie asked.

"I think they're safer staying in one spot."

The same slimy snake demon from earlier slithered toward them, snapping its fangs and hissing. The creature lunged for Walter's ankle.

"Look out!" Charlie kicked the demon, launching it across the room.

"Nice one!" Walter cheered. "Thanks!"

"No problem."

As the demons began to thin out, those remaining scanned the locker room desperately searching for an escape. But three of the Agents had already set up another shield blocking the path to the rear exit. With nowhere to go, the creatures bristled, ready to take down as many Agents as they could with them.

"*Stop!*" Wisdom's voice rose above the noise.

The room filled with a throbbing purple light from Wisdom's Celestial stone, and the fighting paused as Agents and Underworld creatures shielded their eyes from its magnificent brilliance.

"You are all intruding on a sanctioned ceremony! I have been given permission to conduct this from Darwin Pollock, Head Assigner of Agents for HLTA. I have a signed document. So stop interfering and leave at once!"

"Darwin's been fired and arrested, you pip-squeak!" Ronald said.

Wisdom wavered on his feet, his eyes homing in on Ronald. "Is that a fact? Well, no matter. The contract is still binding!"

"Darwin acted on his own accord. That contract has no power over our actions!" Teague said.

"Yeah? Well, I happen to know that this *stone* of mine has power over your actions. It's powerful enough to destroy everyone and everything in this room. I'm going to finish this ceremony, and none of you are going to stop me! Don't think I won't zap you into oblivion!" he shouted as one of the Agents took a step toward him. Wisdom held out the stone, and more light, even brighter than before, swirled around it.

"Psst," Walter whispered to get Charlie's attention. He looked at Wisdom to check if the coast was clear, and squared his shoulders. "Wish me luck."

"Luck?" Charlie asked. "Luck with what?"

Walter winked.

50

A Familiar Voice

The squadron of Agents braced themselves. The remaining demons, backed up against the lockers, tried to shout a warning. But Wisdom wasn't listening to anyone, and he wasn't paying attention to anything going on behind him either. As he flashed the stone, threatening to destroy anyone, Agent or demon, that came close, Walter dove headfirst into his back and possessed him.

For the second time in his short tenure as a rookie Agent, Walter found himself trapped in someone else's body.

Wisdom shivered, and his hand faltered for a second, nearly dropping the stone. "What was that? Did anyone else feel that?"

No one answered. A massive, Muppet-like demon held up a finger as though he was about to try to explain. Instead, he shook his head and looked away.

"Never mind." Wisdom batted his hand at the air. "Charlie, start the passage from the beginning, and this time, complete the ceremony! The rest of you, if you're lucky, I'll let you—"

"Hello, Arnold Featherstone." Walter's voice spoke from inside Wisdom's head. "Bet you didn't see *this* coming."

Wisdom squealed in surprise and spun around, the Celestial stone extended. "Where are you?" He peered over Charlie's shoulder. "You can't hide from me!"

"I'm not hiding," Walter said. "I'm right here."

Wisdom whirled back to face the demons huddled against the lockers. "I don't like trickery. I'll make you suffer if you don't show yourself this instant!"

"That's going to be kind of difficult at the moment."

"And why is that?" Wisdom smiled cruelly; then his face fell.

"Yep," said Walter. "Possession. Not my favorite hobby, but you do what you gotta do. And right now, I gotta teach you a lesson."

Using his strength and remembering what Ronald had told him in Tyrone Underhill's neighborhood, Walter focused his energy on holding the Celestial stone in Wisdom's hand. If he succeeded in touching the stone from inside Wisdom, he would set off the stone's self-destruct mechanism.

Walter squeezed, and the stone began to tremble. Cracks appeared along the surface, and white light seeped through the openings.

"What are you doing? That's mine! You can't do that!" Wisdom insisted. "You're going to break it!"

But Walter held tight. The Celestial stone shook violently. Walter's entire body vibrated, and his teeth chattered together. Then every sound was sucked from the room.

Absolute silence.

A few of the demons dropped their claws from shielding their eyes and stared around the room in confusion.

"That's it?" Walter looked at the stone and then at Ronald. "I thought you said it would—"

Kaboom!

The stone exploded, showering light, dust, and what looked like purple flames over every soul, living, dead, or demon, in the room. The sound rattled Walter's teeth, and his eardrums threatened to pop. Debris swirled around in a purple vortex, uprooting demons, large and small, from their hiding places as they swirled within the vortex and crashed into the walls and lockers. One by one, the monsters in the room disappeared in puffs of smoke.

The Summoner's Handbook began to rock on the floor, then floated into the air, spinning in a page-rattling circle. With a hissing pop, the book vanished, leaving behind only a small pile of ash as evidence of its existence.

Wisdom stared at his empty, upturned hand and screamed. The book was gone. His Celestial stone was no more. In its place, a miniature mushroom cloud rose up from his palm, leaving behind an enormous, throbbing blister.

Walter checked the others. All the Agents had survived, and Charlie's parents and Melissa were still tied up and physically intact.

Charlie rushed over and began working on Melissa's bindings.

"Sorry I got you mixed up in all this," he said. He sounded like a hero in a movie!

"No problem." She flashed him a smile.

Teague approached Wisdom, who collapsed to his knees.

"I was tricked! You can't punish me because I was bamboozled by one of your own kind! It's not my fault," he spluttered. "I'm innocent. Anyone in my position would've acted in a similar manner. You have to see that! You have to grant me mercy!"

The chiseled Agent stared at the wretched man in front of him. "You ready, Walter?"

Walter took a deep breath. "Ready."

Taking his Energy Transfer Device from his utility belt, Teague attached the padded ends of two thin wires to Wisdom's temples and flipped a switch. Both Wisdom and Walter howled in pain as the effects of the possession reversed. Walter's body flew out of Wisdom's. Woozy, disoriented, and shaking erratically, he plopped down on the floor next to Charlie.

"That was awesome!" Walter said. "Never try that at home. Luckily, I'm a professional."

Wisdom made a sound like a booming hiccup, his teeth chattering, arms and legs trembling. When the shaking stopped, he returned to groveling at Teague's feet.

"Surely you can overlook this little disturbance. My intentions were just, if a little misguided. But I can fix all the wrongs I made. I have money! Power! I can do so much good!"

What a pathetic sight, Walter thought. Wisdom had stooped so low. Walter couldn't wait to hear what kind of punishment was in store for him.

"Untie the humans," Teague ordered.

"Absolutely! Of course!" Wisdom scrambled to his feet

and untied the bindings on Charlie's parents. Mr. and Mrs. Dewdle stayed quiet as they stared around the room in disbelief. Charlie had finished with Melissa's binding and was helping her to her feet. She too gaped around the room, but her expression was filled with wonder and excitement.

Charlie, wearing a goofy grin, moved closer to Walter.

"What?" Walter asked. "What's so funny?"

"I'm taller than you," he said as he peered over the top of Walter's head.

"We should go," Teague said. "Walter, we need to get you back to the Academy for debriefing. There's a lot we need to know before the hearing."

"Hearing?" Walter looked at Teague. "What hearing?"

"Darwin's standing trial in a few hours, and we need to walk you through what you're going to say."

Charlie's mom wrapped her arm around his shoulder. "When did the police arrive?" she asked, staring at each of the uniformed Agents. "I must say, they do look handsome in white."

Charlie's dad glanced sideways at his wife and spoke out of the corner of his mouth. "I don't think they're the police, dear."

"What are you guys, angels or something?" Melissa covered her mouth and squealed. "Oh my gosh! You are, aren't you?"

"Interesting," Teague said. "It would appear that you three, along with Charlie, have developed the sight. I suppose this is a result of the Celestial stone explosion. I'll be sure to log that in the report. Now, after you." He held his hand out toward the exit, and the Dewdles quickly obeyed, but not before Charlie's mom had time to pause and squeeze her son in a bear hug. Glancing at the others, she acknowledged Walter standing somewhat timidly beside Charlie.

"It's nice to finally meet you, Walter." She reached over to grab Walter's arm. Her hand effortlessly passed through as though he were made of smoke. "Oh my." Charlie's mom swallowed, and Charlie's dad had to lead her along up the stairs.

Melissa, Charlie, and Walter fell in line behind the Dewdles, followed by the other Agents.

"Hey, wait a minute," Walter said. "Teague, what about Willows? We're not just going to leave him here, are we?"

Wisdom still stood in the corner of the locker room, wringing the cut ropes in his hands like a wet towel. He smiled sheepishly at Teague, then glared at Walter.

"What do you expect us to do?" Teague asked.

"Punish him!" Charlie said. "He can't get away with this. Not after all he's done! We need to lock him up."

"I agree wholeheartedly. But where do you suggest we do so? He's not dead. And unfortunately, the Afterlife Academy is forbidden to assist with that process."

"Then send him to a regular prison. At least call the cops and let them know what he did!"

"What did he do exactly?" Teague asked.

"Are you kidding?" Walter said.

"He almost opened a demonic Gateway!" Charlie exclaimed.

"And are you willing to hold to that testimony in a human

court of law?" Teague smiled. "How do you think that would go? Would any of the authorities believe you? What proof could you show them?"

"But—but—" Charlie looked pleadingly at Walter.

"He had to have broken at least *some* human laws to-night," Walter reasoned. "Kidnapping, for starters."

"True," Teague conceded. "He did hold Charlie and his family prisoner for about three hours. That might get him a year in a minimum-security prison. But considering the amount of wealth he's amassed, Wisdom could buy his way out in less time. Everything else witnessed here and all that he's done by aiding and abetting the demons would never hold up in court."

"So that's it?" Charlie couldn't believe it. Wisdom, the pathetic weasel, would just get off scot-free?

"I'm afraid there's nothing *we* can do." Teague gave Charlie a meaningful look. "Come along now."

After giving one final glance around the room to re-member the destruction that had taken place only moments earlier, Walter and Charlie exited the locker room, leaving behind a puzzled Wisdom Willows scratching his head in a stupor.

51

Salinger's Ghost

Standing in front of his video camera, Charlie pointed at the hole by his feet. Behind him, the crumpled walls of the abandoned shopping mall blotted out the setting sun and cast shadows across the construction site. The dim light normally would make it difficult to film, but not with Charlie's new camera. The expensive piece of equipment could operate day or night with maximum performance. The state-of-the-art lenses were guaranteed not to smudge, and they recorded everything in high definition. The video camera was a gift from his parents. They felt it was the least they could do after Charlie had saved the world.

"As you can see, the readings on my EMF detector are off the charts." Charlie pointed to another brand-new piece of equipment as he spoke to the camera. Green lights blinked and chirped across the screen. "When Friedman Salinger took refuge here in this unmarked grave"—he held up a hand and gestured to the air around him—"he only intended to remain hidden long enough for Sheriff Mockley and his posse to pass by. But when the ground unexpectedly shifted, shaking Colton County with a magnitude six-point-five earthquake, this unmarked burial plot became the final resting place of the notorious Colton County strangler."

Charlie stared grimly into the camera. "As many paranormal researchers will tell you, whenever a brutal killer dies from an unexplained phenomenon, he doesn't go quietly. And because of the nature in which he died, buried alive by an earthquake, Friedman Salinger's soul was trapped in this grave. Now, for the first time ever, I will capture on video evidence of Friedman Salinger's ghost." He pointed down into the hole.

Walter Prairie blinked up at him. "Do I really have to do this?" he asked in a bored voice.

Charlie's eyes widened, and he raised his eyebrows expectantly. "Any second now, folks, you will see proof!"

"Really? This is so stupid," Walter groaned.

"Any second now!" Charlie said again.

Walter puffed out his cheeks and removed a device from his utility belt. After mashing a few codes on a keypad, he pointed the small piece of equipment at one of the dirt walls of the hole and pressed a button.

"Oh my," Charlie said in dramatic fashion as purple waves of energy bounced off the wall. "Did you see that?" Dirt clods and rocks tumbled from the side of the hole. Charlie gasped. "And that?" Insects burrowed out and skittered up to the ground. "Friedman's spirit is *very* angry!"

"Wahoo," Walter said, twirling a finger next to his head. "It's unbelievable!" After a few seconds of capturing trembling dirt and crawling insects, Walter clicked off the device and pocketed it in his belt.

"There you have it, ladies and gentlemen." Charlie turned once more to face the camera. "Fact or fiction? Does Friedman Salinger haunt the earth still, trapped in an earthly prison? You be the judge."

"And cut!" Melissa announced as she pressed "stop" on the camcorder. "That was really good, Charlie. You sounded very convincing."

"Really?" Charlie blushed. "It took me two days to remember those lines."

"*Two days?* Try all week!" Walter clambered out of the hole. "I had to put in a request to the Academy for specialized earplugs!"

After Walter's debriefing with Teague and the other Agents, he had to stand as a witness in Darwin Pollock's trial. Instead of wearing his usual three-piece suit, Darwin graced the courtroom in a striking purple jumpsuit with a white ID number stamped on the back. The trial went on for several days, as Darwin's legal team proved to be sharp. In the end, though, Walter's testimony sealed the deal. No one in their right mind could forgive Darwin for so endangering Walter by putting him into the field without so much as an hour of training, let alone the requisite four years.

Darwin's conviction created a highly coveted job opportunity as the Head Assigner of Agents for HLTA at the Afterlife Academy. Though many qualified individuals applied, Alton Tremonton finally earned his promotion.

His first order of business: figuring out what to do with Walter.

The Logan brothers had returned to their assigned targets and were now enjoying all the fun of being full-fledged Agents. To Walter, it didn't seem fair that he'd have to be stuck in the Academy for four years. After almost nonstop begging on Walter's part, Alton agreed to meet him at his office with a surprise.

Walter's first "official" assignment.

He would have to return to the Academy regularly to undergo training classes, but Alton concluded that Walter's experience guarding *The Summoner's Handbook* had proven his value in the field. Charlie might no longer have been in possession of the dangerous book, but that didn't mean he was completely safe. Charlie couldn't simply foil a demon takeover and then disappear from the Underworld radar for the rest of his life. Revenge was always a possibility. So, when not in class, Walter served as Charlie's Afterlife Academy Agent.

"You don't think I overdid the details of Salinger's murders, do you?" Charlie asked Melissa once they had returned every piece of his equipment to its slot in his carrying case.

"No, it was just the right amount. Creepy, but not disgusting," she replied.

"That's good. I still think I need to buy some makeup or something to help my face not look so pale. All the professionals do that."

"Don't buy anything. I have some makeup at home, and whatever else we need, I'll just borrow from my sister." Melissa brushed the hair from her eyes. "But I wouldn't worry about that, either. I think you have the right look for this documentary."

Charlie grinned and felt his face flush.

"Oh my gosh! Could we be done now?" Walter glanced from Charlie to Melissa.

"Yeah, I better get going," Melissa said. "If I don't leave now, I'll be late for cheer practice."

Along with Charlie and his parents, Melissa maintained her ability to see Walter, along with any other Agent who happened to check in on Charlie. It was a side effect from the Celestial stone explosion, and no one at the Academy had any idea how long it would last. They could see the Underworld creatures as well. Fortunately, the demons were licking their wounds and staying away for the moment, and Charlie and Walter had only spotted the occasional shade floating by the neighborhood.

"Thanks again for helping with the video," Charlie said.

"It was fun! I'll see you tomorrow." Melissa waved and walked away briskly.

Now that his documentary was finished, Charlie had a difficult decision to make. Which website was he going to submit it to? He checked SpiritSpy.org daily with the intent of keeping tabs on Wisdom Willows, but the site hadn't resumed operations in over a month. It was as if Wisdom had simply vanished.

Life at Cunningham Middle School continued, but it wasn't exactly back to normal. Charlie's popularity had waned once the novelty of his victory over Mo had worn off, but Mo and his thugs seemed to have permanently laid off. Especially now that Melissa Bitner was constantly hanging out at Charlie's locker and sitting next to him in the cafeteria.

Even if Mo had still been bothering him, Charlie didn't

think he'd have minded like before. He had helped save the world from a demon takeover. Mo's empty threats and insults were tiny in comparison. Plus, in a battle of wits and words with opponents like Mo and Wheeler, Charlie knew he always had the upper hand, especially with friends like Walter and Melissa by his side.

"Now can we finally go do something *I* want to do?" Walter asked.

Charlie sighed. "I guess, but I have to feed my birds first. You know how cranky Doris gets if she misses a meal."

"Give me a break. They should just be grateful they weren't dog food. I still can't believe they all found their way back."

Charlie agreed. Of all the strange things that had happened to him recently, he considered his birds' homecoming to be the biggest miracle.

"It'll just take me a few minutes to feed them." Charlie slung the strap of his video-camera bag over his shoulder. "What do you want to do, anyways?"

Walter tapped his lip with his finger and thought. "Hmmm . . . I don't know. Something fun. Something exciting. Something . . ."

"We're not sneaking into Melissa's cheer practice again, so you can just forget about it."

Walter clutched his chest as though Charlie had said something incredibly hurtful. A wry grin stretched across his face. "I'm shocked you would even suggest that."

52

A Champion at Last

Trutti's eyes gleamed as he eagerly rubbed his hands together and pulled a bone from the tower. A smart choice. The tower remained intact, and Trutti's face radiated pure joy as he grinned at his master. Hoonga offered him an approving nod, and Trutti erupted in a fit of giggles.

The game of Bones had never gone in this direction before. He had played it with Hoonga thousands of times, and each round had always proven painful for the lesser demon. Burned ears. Scorched eyes. Boiled fingers and toes. The amount of pain Trutti had endured over the years could not possibly be measured.

Now the tables had turned. He had won seven games in a row. The next piece selected would topple the tower, and it wasn't Trutti's turn to pick. He was about to add another win to his name.

Hoonga stared at the tower, aware of this fact. He clapped his hands and a look of pride etched his demonic features.

"Your move, Arnold," the giant demon announced. Hoonga's eye narrowed as he glared down upon the third participant in the game of Bones. "Might as well get it over with."

Wisdom Willows sat strapped to one of the chairs in the outpost office. His green robe was torn and tattered, and his watery eyes looked exhausted. "Do I have to?" he whimpered.

Hoonga glanced at Trutti for approval, and the bat-eared demon nodded enthusiastically.

"I'm afraid so," Hoonga said. "Hurry up, please. We need to restack the tower so we can play another game."

"Another game? How many are we going to play?" Wisdom's voice cracked.

"So many!" Trutti shouted. "Hundreds! Thousands! Bones is the best game ever!"

Wisdom's chin dropped. "But I don't want to play anymore. I'm so tired. Please, let's just stop!"

Hoonga's lower lip curled, and he wore an empathetic expression. "Very well," he said with a sigh. "We'll stop after this round."

Trutti stomped his foot. "*Awwww!* No way!" Hoonga giving in to the begging of a human? That wasn't like him at all. Trutti folded his arms and stuck out his tongue. "That's not fair, and you know it!"

"Come on, Trutti, don't be like that," Hoonga purred. "We can try another game for a little while. I'll even let you pick. What would be a fun activity we all three could enjoy?" Hoonga smiled, and the two demons stared across the room at a familiar deck of playing cards. Trutti flipped onto his back and clapped his feet together vigorously. Hoonga roared with laughter.

Wisdom raised his head and followed their gaze to see what had spurred their excitement, just as Trutti began to chant.

"Old Maid! Old Maid! Old Maid!"

Acknowledgments

With most books, or at least the ones I have written, the author is just one of the many pieces working together that makes a story come to life. Yes, my name may end up on the cover, but that's only because there would be too many names to include if we did it differently.

Over the years, my wife, Heidi, has given me support and confidence, and perhaps most importantly, time to write. She sacrifices so much because she believes in me.

I owe a ton to Shannon Hassan, my phenomenal agent at Marsal Lyon Literary Agency. She took a chance on my work when I thought no one would. She truly is amazing!

It has been an absolute dream come true working with Delacorte Press and Random House and especially my editor, Rebecca Weston. She is so brilliant and has such vision and patience. Perhaps she knows my characters better than I do. Also, many thanks to Michelle Poploff, who first pulled the lever that allowed this ball to start rolling.

Thank you to Lisa Weber and to the Delacorte Press design team, particularly Katrina Damkoehler, for creating an amazing cover. Lisa somehow managed to pluck the images of my characters straight out of my mind. That *is* Charlie and Walter!

This story has been through many revisions since the idea was conceived over four years ago, and I am indebted to anyone who took a glance at it and steered me in the right direction. These readers include Jennifer Judd, Ethan Judd, Michael Cole, Taylor Fleming, Susan LaDuke, B. K. Bostick, Kevin Lemley, James Loveless, Nichole Giles, Amy Grow, and Jackson Cole.

Thank you to my family: my parents, for their encouragement, and my children, Jackson, Gavin, and Camberlyn, for being my guinea pigs. You all are the reason I write.

Lastly, a booming thanks goes to you, my readers, for trying out this book. Your time is so valuable and you have countless books to fill it with, and yet somehow you chose mine. I hope I didn't let you down.

About the Author

Frank L. Cole lives with his wife and three children out west. Over the years, he has seen his share of wraiths and shades, but thankfully, no banshees just yet. When he's not writing books or dodging demons, Frank enjoys going to the movies and traveling. *The Afterlife Academy* is Frank's eighth published book. His Guardian Agent's name is Rolph.

You can learn more about his writing at franklewiscole .blogspot.com.